I0628009

USA TODAY BESTSELLING AUTHOR

SARAH BRIANNE

DANTE

MADE MEN

Young Ink Press Publication
YoungInkPress.com

Copyright © 2025 by Sarah Brianne

Edited by CD Editing
and Diamond in the Rough Editing
Cover Art by Young Ink Press

All rights reserved.

No part of this book may be reproduced in any form or by any electronic or
mechanical means including information storage and retrieval systems,
without permission in writing from the author. The only exception is by a
reviewer, who may quote short excerpts in a review.

This book is a work of fiction. Names, characters, places, and incidents
either are products of the author's imagination or are used fictitiously. Any
resemblance to actual persons, living or dead, events, or locales is entirely
coincidental.

Connect with Sarah,
facebook.com/AuthorSarahBrianne
instagram.com/authorsarahbrianne
youtube.com/sarahbrianne-author
tiktok.com/@authorsarahbrianne
SarahBrianne.com

PROLOGUE

DARK FAMILY TIES

"Haley, all I'm asking you to do is to take one meeting for me. Is that too much to ask from you?" It was. It truly was. Her poor reclusive friend could barely order a cup of coffee with confidence, much less expect her to do what she was asking of her now. But Nadia had to convince her co-partner to do this somehow. Her charity depended on it, and it was now solely resting on Haley's shoulders.

Nadia slapped down two manila folders on the desk, each containing her best friend's worst nightmare.

Watching her put on her glasses, she could see Haley's confidence sink when the names on the folders came into focus.

After a few moments of silence, Nadia snapped her manicured fingers in front of her ashen face. "Earth calling Haley."

"I'm sorry ..."

"Forget whatever excuse you were about to give me. It's not going to work this time." Laying her palms on the desk, Nadia moved closer to face Haley. They had known each other since they were thirteen, and she had given her every weak excuse in the fucking book. Sometimes, Nadia would pity her and accept it, but today was not one of those days. "I can't be at two meetings in different areas of the city at the same time. We need the funding to find a new building. We have less than two months to find something with the space and the facilities we need ..." It was time for her to hit below the belt. "Or the kids are going to be back on the streets. Do you want that?"

"You know I don't!" Haley started to lose it as she was slowly being cornered with no way out. "I suck at doing this type of stuff. Just reschedule!"

"I've tried!" Nadia stated the obvious. Asking the scaredy cat was clearly her last resort. "I'm worried that, if I try again, they'll change their minds about giving us a chance to solicit their donations. I can't become a nuisance before they even meet me."

The two meetings dealt with two different millionaires who, unfortunately, could only meet at the same designated time. Over a hundred thousand dollars were on the line, along with the countless lives of at-risk teens. As much as she loved Haley and tried to keep her in her little bubble as much as possible, Nadia would pop it in a heartbeat for the kids. *Haley would live ... right?*

Seeing the eyes behind her huge glasses move back to the names, Nadia knew she broke her and started to feel a twinge of guilt. This charity was her baby, and her baby for a reason. They both knew Haley had come along for a smooth ride. She had given her the position of accountant so she could handle things behind the scenes where she felt comfortable. Nadia, however, was the face of it now, after she had taken it over from her beloved Anna.

"Desmond Beck ..." Haley read one of the names before

4

reading the name on the second folder. "Dante Caruso." Swallowing hard, she pushed her fallen glasses higher up the bridge of her nose as she looked back up at Nadia. "Why do they sound like they're both in the mafia?"

Well, this is awkward ... "I think one actually is," she mumbled under her breath, hoping her friend couldn't hear.

"*Nadia!*" she exasperated shakily.

She held up a finger. "Remember the children."

Haley rubbed her temple. "Fine. Just tell me which one that is."

Nadia moved her finger to the folder that held Dante's name for a split-second before the other folder was snatched up and claimed by greedy little hands.

"I am *so* not getting involved in those dark *family* ties," Haley said with a shiver, looking at the folder that still lay on the table.

"I don't blame you," Nadia told her sympathetically, knowing her friend came from dark family ties of her own. "But, um ..." *Ugh*, this was going to suck to tell her this. "Don't be angry, but I had to use your family connection to even get an appointment with Desmond Beck."

If it was possible, Haley's face dropped even more. "Which family connection?"

Nadia had to avert her eyes. "I couldn't even reach Mr. Beck's assistant to ask for an appointment until I mentioned your family name and that you're related to George and Amelia Clark."

Haley's eyes went as big as her glasses. "I haven't talked to my uncle and cousin in years."

"He doesn't know that, does he?" she said slyly, but the guilt panged in her chest again. Picking up the untouched folder, she held it out to her. "We can still switch, if you would like?"

Haley eyed it like it suddenly looked like the better option. "How mafia are we talking? Robert De Niro or Al Pacino?"

"Would it really matter?" she asked her honestly.

"Robert De Niro is actually capable of having a kind face," Haley stated the difference before the brave face she had put on slowly disappeared. "But what does Desmond Beck do again?"

"He's just a philanthropist." *Well, I hope.* She kept that bit to herself this time.

Haley's orbs danced between the folder in her hand and the one Nadia still held out, clearly trying to decide the lesser of two evils. "I'll go with my gut instinct." She gripped her folder tighter, solidifying her fate with Desmond.

"All right." Nadia brought the folder closer to her, staring down at the name *Dante Caruso*. Unlike Haley, her fate had just been decided for her. An ominous shiver went up her back.

Putting on a brave face herself, she held her folder to her own chest. "There, that wasn't so hard, was it?"

"Clearly, you have put your blinders on. You know I can't get three words out in a row on a good day, much less when I'm nervous."

"I'll write down everything you need to say. Just memorize the script I give you." Nadia already solved that problem. "You got this."

A quiet sigh of defeat escaped Haley's lips.

"You'll see ..." Nadia no longer knew who she was trying to convince anymore.

"Are you sure there isn't a way that you can at least come with me to start the meeting then leave?" Clearly, this was Haley's last-ditch effort.

"I won't be able to start the meeting with you, but ..." Nadia gave in to her guilt, "if mine finishes early, then I *may* be able to take over the meeting from you."

Haley looked relieved as she bounced her head in a nod. "Then let's go with that plan."

"Plan?" Nadia had taken pity on her, and it was already backfiring. "It's not a plan. It's a *maybe!*"

Smiling, Haley pushed her glasses up again. "I'll hold down the fort until you can get there. This will work much better ..." Haley nervously spoke the words that would most certainly jinx them. "What could go wrong?"

The two women stared at each other, unaware that the same thought was now going through both their minds.

A million things.

ALL RICH ASSHOLES ARE THE SAME

Nadia hated casinos ... No, she *loathed* casinos. Not only were they greedy businesses that preyed on the weak, but they were loud as hell and reeked of smoke. If Haley was in her hell, currently on the other side of Kansas City, Nadia was definitely in hers.

She came up to a huge security guard dressed in a basic black suit who appeared to have been expecting her since he immediately led her into the elevator and punched in a few buttons for different floors that seemed to be a code to take them straight to the top.

The guard wasn't much for conversing, as the awkward silence filled the air for a quick moment. Getting off the elevator, she followed closely behind the suited man. Now, Nadia wasn't the nervous type, but she was starting to feel like taking a meeting with a potential mob boss might have been a bad idea.

The guard knocked on a door with a heavy fist.

A dark voice sounded from the other side. "Come in."

She watched him open the door, and it wasn't until the

huge man stepped to the side to let her enter the office that she was able to see into the room.

Oh God. Nadia swallowed.

"Thank you, Amo," Dante dismissed him.

Nadia would have only moments until the guard left and closed her into his office for her to gather her thoughts and screw her head back on straight. The man before her was definitely no Robert De Niro ... or Al Pacino. Even though he was an older gentleman, probably in his late forties, he was breathtakingly handsome. Hell, if she was honest, his age was what made him even more so. Any girl with daddy issues—and Nadia was one—would be risking it all for one night in his bed.

His dark, tanned skin glowed next to his expensive black suit jacket and white button-up dress shirt. He only had a little bit of speckling gray through his pitch-black hair, but it weirdly made him hotter. It was his piercing icy-blue eyes, however, that had her unable to breathe until the door snapped closed behind her and her time of being jumbled up was over.

"Mr. Caruso," she got right to business, "thank you for seeing m—"

"I'm afraid we don't have much time," he said, looking at his watch before he waved to the chair in front of his desk. "Please sit, Mrs. Brooks."

"*Ms.* Brooks," she corrected him.

There seemed to be a slight surprise behind those icy eyes of his before it quickly vanished. "I apologize, Ms. Brooks." Again, he repeated with another wave, "Sit."

Nadia couldn't help but notice how he told her to sit like it was a command. It was glaringly obvious the man didn't like to repeat himself, and even though she had only just met him, he appeared to always get what he wanted.

Taking the seat, she didn't need to see the future to know that this wasn't going to go the way she had planned. Hell, he hadn't even bothered to get out of his leather chair, or shake her hand, much less give her more than a few-second glance. That last part might have hurt her womanly pride, but she had to remind herself that she wasn't here for that. Nadia was here for the children, and she wasn't going to go down easily. Seeing that time was an issue, she got right to it.

"I'm here on behalf of my charity, Moonbeam. We are—"

"Do you mind?" he asked nonchalantly, holding up an unlit cigar.

She, in fact, did mind, but before she could answer, he was already lighting the end; not that she had room for complaint as it was his office.

"No," she grumbled out before continuing. "We are looking to upgrade our facility." She watched him blow out a puff of smoke as he stared at his rich cigar more than he was paying any attention to her. Still, she managed to trot on. "With that, we can help house more at-risk teens throughout all of Kansas Ci ..." She trailed off as she noticed him glance at his watch. Fury rose inside her. "I'm sorry. Do you have somewhere to be?"

"Actually, yes," he answered with harsh honesty. "Your incessant calls have, unfortunately, driven me to finally accept this meeting. I specifically agreed to today because I'm taking my youngest son on vacation for the weekend."

Unfortunately, *all rich assholes are the same.*

"Then, by all means, Mr. Caruso ... let me get right to it." But she did have to give him credit for the smart play of not letting this meeting drag along. "I'd like a generous donation from you."

"Don't you all," he muttered under his breath before putting the cigar back to his lips.

Excuse me? Nadia opened her mouth to rip the mother-effer a new one when the door behind her flew open.

"Sir, Leo is in the car, waiting for you out front."

"Sorry, Ms. Brooks, but it looks like this meeting has to be cut short. The yacht will be departing soon," Dante said with a smile, putting out his cigar in the crystal ashtray.

Fucking prick. She wished she had said the insult out loud as she stood from her chair. She didn't plan to waste another bated breath on him, yet she found herself turning to face him one last time.

"I can't believe I was so wrong about you. Have a lovely vacation with your son, Mr. Caruso." There was no hiding the disappointment in her voice. "I'll see myself out," she told the guard who had brought her up and was holding the door open as she passed him.

Having the final word made her feel better ... Slightly, at least. *Of course, the vacation he's going on is on his fucking yacht,* she thought to herself as she walked back the way she had come. While she was desperately trying to fight for her kids, who didn't have a dime to their names, Dante was taking his probably just as stuck-up son on a vacation that most likely wasn't a drop in the bucket of his wealth. Nadia couldn't believe she had found the unbearable man attractive at first. Hitting the elevator button, she began to lie to herself ...

He's freaking hideou—
Speaking of the devil ...

I CAN'T BELIEVE SHE SAID THAT TO ME, WAS THE ONLY thing that had run through Dante's mind for the last minute. He had also told himself that it was his son waiting out front that had him rushing to the elevator.

Seeing her shocked yet frustrated face, he could only imagine the words Nadia was saying about him in her mind.

The curve of Dante's lip lifted up into a devilish smile that he could tell only infuriated her more.

Fueling her imagination gave him pleasure. It had been a long time since a woman had shown him any attitude. The effect he had on women was much like how Nadia had acted the moment she had met him. She had been taken aback by his good looks, but he had been amused with how rapidly she had put it behind her. His effect didn't usually wear off so quickly, *if ever*.

Putting his eyes on the elevator door, Dante supposed the woman was good-looking, too, but it had been even longer since he had found a woman beautiful.

YEP, HE WAS DEFINITELY NOT HIDEOUS. *AT LEAST ON the outside, but his insides sure are.*

Ding. The elevator slid open.

He did his pretend polite wave again. "After you, Ms. Brooks."

As if getting massively turned down wasn't embarrassing enough, she clicked her heels inside the moving box that she was going to have to share with the man who had just brushed her off and took her meeting simply so she would never contact him again.

Dante, followed by his guard, entered the elevator with

her, and then the guard punched in the code to take them straight to the bottom.

With the door sliding closed, Nadia slithered her eyes over to see him staring at his expensive watch again. It was everything she could do to keep her mouth shut, and it was only staying glued that way because she had still had the last word.

Putting his arm back to his side, Dante looked up at the falling numbers.

Nadia snapped her eyes to do the same, unable to wait for her release. Her eyes had wanted to drift back, swearing that she felt the icy gaze of his on her ...

Don't ask.

He wanted to.

I don't care.

He did.

Don't you dare ask.

He definitely wanted to.

I do not fucking care why she said that.

He definitely did, and if he was going to ask, he needed to do it now before ...

Ding.

Oh, thank God.

Relieved, Nadia hurriedly stomped out of the elevator, leaving him in her dust. Well, she hoped, because she wouldn't dare turn her head to see. Nope, her head stayed firmly forward as she went through the casino. Breathing in the cigarette smoke was a relief compared to the scent she'd had to endure in the elevator. The confined space made her realize, with the slight hint of what smelled like whiskey and his expensive cologne, she didn't hate the scent of cigar smoke. Nadia was sure that scent would linger in her mind for days.

Finally, true freedom reached her when she swung open the heavy glass doors. Or so she thought.

She hadn't made it a few steps on the sidewalk, toward her building that was only a few blocks away, when she heard her name being called from that commanding voice.

"Ms. Brooks."

She was tempted to not turn around, but she found her body stopping and turning to look at Mr. Caruso, who stood beside the blacked-out town car that was parked in front of the hotel casino.

"How were you wrong about me?" He spoke loudly so his voice would travel over the noise of the city to her ears. "Because I can't imagine what you expected from a man like me."

Nadia could see his dark features become darker as she stalked up to him. "Yes, I've heard the rumors about you, Mr. Caruso." She made no effort to conceal that she wasn't scared, whether he was or wasn't what those whispers were saying about him. Frankly, she just didn't care what kind of organization he was running, legal or illegal. "But, depending upon who you ask, you're considered a good man in the eyes of a lot people who live in this city."

He seemed to be stunned by her answer for a moment. "The company you keep may not be of your best interest, then, Ms. Brooks."

"The only company I care about are the kids who walk the streets all alone at night and grew up without a fighting chance." She paused for a moment, her warm brown eyes boring into his cold ones. "I was under the impression you helped a young man in that same position once upon a time ..."

DANTE'S JAW FLEXED INTO A HARD POSITION UPON hearing just how much she knew about him. Taking Salvatore Lastra off the streets when he had been just thirteen years old wasn't something a lot of people in Kansas City knew about him. Nadia had clearly done her research, and he didn't know how he should feel about it ... until he did.

SHE WATCHED HIS JAW FIX INTO POSITION AS EVERY hair on her body stood in fear. Men never made their money by being nice, and Nadia was afraid she had just gone too far, especially with Dante, who didn't try hard to pretend he hadn't made his money outside of the law.

"Careful, Ms. Brooks," he warned in a low tone before the curve of his lips went up in another slow smile, "you may find a secret about me one day that you wish you hadn't."

It wasn't until he reached into his hidden suit jacket pocket and pulled out a checkbook and pen that she relaxed.

Oh, I don't doubt it.

Watching him scribble on the check, she couldn't help but think, as soon as she got the check in her greedy little hands, this would be the first and last time she would ever be in the presence of Dante Caruso. She would take all future checks via mail or not fucking at all.

"Thank you, Mr. Caruso," she said sincerely, uncaring of any amount he wrote in that tiny box. But when he handed it to her, she couldn't help but notice it was the exact amount she needed from him. *One hundred thousand dollars.* "Y-you have no idea what this means to us," she stammered in disbelief, pressing the check to her chest.

Placing his checkbook and pen back in his pocket, he threw open the car's back door as his smile disappeared. "Well, the IRS was going to take it from me, anyway."

Nadia wanted to roll her eyes at him, but she could see past what he was trying to pull off. Keeping up his asshole façade must have been tiring.

"I don't care," she told him honestly, putting the check in her blazer pocket before holding out her slender hand. "Thank you, Mr. Caruso."

He stared at her hand for a moment before he took it in his. "You're welcome."

All focus had been lost again as his hand touched hers and she went right back to how she felt when she had first seen him in his office. "H-Have a lovely trip," Nadia told him genuinely this time, not wanting his contact with her dropped anytime soon.

If he felt even remotely the way she did, he was much better at concealing his emotions. "Have a lovely day, Ms. Brooks."

She felt his grip loosen, and her heart sank until his grip suddenly tightened on hers again, this time in a death grip. Everything seemed to move in fast motion as she was then thrown into the back seat of his car.

However ... it didn't seem to happen fast enough.

BANG!

SPOILER ALERT ... THE RUMORS
ABOUT DANTE CARUSO ARE TRUE

S*hit, shit, shit,* was all Dante thought as he slammed their bodies into the back seat of the car. He couldn't explain it. It had just been a gut feeling that he needed to get out of the way, and fast. His instincts taking Ms. Brooks with him.

"Get us the fuck out of here!" he growled.

Amo had already thrown the car in drive. "On it."

The car being punched forward, which threw the back-seat car door to an automatic close. Dante was thankful that, while he had been talking to Ms. Brooks, Amo was getting into the driver's seat. One of his soldiers, Vincent, had driven Leo up, and they would all be fucked if he was the one driving them away from this shit show. Amo was one of his few men left who wasn't stuck up a girl's ass, so he was one of the only ones he trusted willing to be his guard for the weekend. It was a dark time for the *family* if his men couldn't leave their women for a few days to go party on a fucking yacht. God, he really missed the old days.

"Leo?" His fatherly instinct had him yelling out for his son.

"I'm fine." Leo's voice came from the passenger side. It seemed to be dropping octaves more and more each day.

Able to focus on the woman in his arms now, he studied her. "Are you hurt?" When she didn't answer, he nervously began checking her body. It was strange, the fear he felt banging in his chest. He hadn't felt fear like that since ...

WHAT THE FUCK! NADIA'S HEART POUNDED IN HER chest. She had wanted to scream, but the shock didn't allow it. Then her shock turned into even more shock, if that was possible, when she felt Dante's hands searching her body for a gunshot wound. She could practically feel the relief radiate off him when he realized the reasoning for her silence.

"Ms. Brooks, I think you're in shock."

Was that a ... s*mirk on his face? What about this is funny?* She was repulsed that her internal monologue was braver than she was on the outside at the moment. It would take her until the fear of imminent death wore off, she supposed.

"Uh-huh," was all she managed with a little nod to confirm that he had hit the nail on the fucking head.

That slight smirk on his face grew a touch bigger as he began to sit up.

"Sir, I'd stay down," Amo said, looking serious in his rearview mirror.

"Why—Oh shit," he groaned when he was thrown back into the seat when a car rammed into their rear end.

"Christ!" Nadia yelled, seeming to have found her voice upon the second hit. The only reason she hadn't gone flying was because the grip Dante had on her was becoming slightly painful at this point.

"Hang on," was the only warning Amo gave before he suddenly jumped on the freeway.

Well, if the car behind them wasn't going to be the one to kill them all, it certainly was going to be the breakneck speed the Caruso bodyguard was sure to impend upon them.

"Why am I getting the feeling this is normal for you three?" she asked, exasperated at being the only one showing any emotion.

She had expected Dante to be the one to answer. Instead, it was his son, Leo, who ominously said, "It is."

Nadia couldn't see much of the boy yet, with Dante's body blocking her sight, but from what she could see, she guessed he was definitely a teenager, and the cut of the dirty blond hair told her that he probably didn't fall far from the tree in the good-looks department. Calling his son pretentious was going to be an understatement if he looked half as good in the front as he did from the back, especially with kids these days.

The back seat of the car was small, anyway, but with her height and fat ass, along with Dante's tall ... firm ... muscular frame, which she had delightfully discovered over the last few minutes of being pressed up against him, only made the seat smaller. She desperately needed a breather.

"Okay, I think it's safe enough to sit up."

Dante's warning wasn't fast enough as she fought to get out from under him. "I wouldn't—"

This time, the three-word phrase had no trouble coming out when a bullet hit the back windshield. "What the fuck!"

"It's bulletproof," he told her, "but it's best not to test it."

"You think?" Sarcasm was an understatement for how

her words came out as she slammed her body back down with Dante's. Bulletproof glass was like airplanes—it was something you couldn't explain how it would even fucking work and only had one explanation. *Witchcraft.*

"I think he just wants to take you out, sir," Amo stated, seeing he and Leo were clearly not the target.

"That bullet *was* meant for me," Dante darkly confirmed. It was clear he didn't have a shadow of a doubt on his mind.

Amo gripped the wheel tighter. "It looks like our friend is done with the games and has decided to go straight to the top."

"*Your friend?*" Gulping, Nadia's mouth slowly started going dry while she stared at Dante. "How many of your men has your friend taken out so far?"

"A few," he admitted after a few passing moments. "And then some."

Nadia didn't know what "*and then some*" meant, but she really didn't like the sound of that. It somehow seemed worse than death.

Seeing the fear flash across her features, he reassured her, "I promise to get you home safely, Ms. Brooks."

Okay, *that* she liked the sound of coming from his hot lips.

"Don't worry, boss,"—Amo took the car to new heights, trying to lose the person following them, for good this time —"I don't plan on any of us dying from One-Shot today."

"*One-Shot?*" Nadia repeated the name drop as if it was casual. Whoever, or whatever, it was that was chasing after them had clearly earned a reputation badass enough to warrant a nickname like that.

I'm fucked, aren't I?

I'M FUCKED AREN'T I? DANTE DIDN'T KNOW HOW TO tell her that One-Shot had gotten his name because he only needed one bullet to shoot someone right between the eyes.

Clearing his throat, he hoped to change the subject. "Leo, get Lucca on the phone—"

Before he could finish, his son had his phone pressed to his ear. "Vincent already told him. He heard the gunshot as he was walking into the casino. He tried to go after the car but lost it. Lucca's been tracking us, but no one's been able to catch up to us."

"Won't matter much now; we lost him," Amo said, glancing sternly into the rearview mirror.

Leo listened to the other end for a few moments before hanging up.

Having mixed feelings about losing One-Shot was an understatement for Dante at the moment. If Leo, or Ms. Brooks, hadn't been in the car, he and Amo would have chanced their luck at taking him out.

"I think it's safe now to sit up," Nadia had to remind him.

"Right." Dante shook his head slightly before muttering, "Sorry."

FEELING HIS GRIP ON HER LOOSEN AND DISAPPEAR, SHE quickly sat up. Her body might've enjoyed being pressed up against him, but her mind was becoming more claustrophobic in this death trap of a car by the second. The sweat on her brow and racing heart had her wondering if she was becoming lightheaded or car sick.

"Can we slow down now?" she asked the crazed driver, whose foot hadn't left the gas.

Amo acted as if he hadn't heard her.

She wiped the bead of sweat that was sliding down her temple, her voice seeming to become weak as she said, "Please."

"Slow down." Dante's order carried strongly to the front of the car and, almost immediately, the car began to slow to a more legal fast speed. "Take your jacket off ..."

Huh? she thought in a haze.

"Before you pass out."

Oh.

WATCHING HER STRUGGLE, HE SCOOTED CLOSER TO HER to help her get her black blazer down her arms. His cold eyes followed the perspiration sliding down the side of her face, to the beads that were beginning to form on her chest. He watched one of the salty beads fall from her clavicle, slowly traveling down to her breasts, before it disappeared under her white tank top that was being revealed.

Dante no longer "supposed" the woman was beautiful, as Nadia was, in fact, beautiful. Her hair was silky black and didn't quite touch her shoulders. He found himself liking the style of it. It was a smart, chic style that suited her bone structure. It was parted to the side, with one side of her hair being fuller than the other, in a bob-like cut. It was the type of haircut only women with strong, beautiful features could pull off.

Being a part of the Italian mafia, it was a bad habit to want to know what ethnicity a person was, as they mostly dealt with people of the same bloodline as themselves, since the beginning of time. He wasn't quite sure what bloodline Nadia had. While they shared many of the same features on paper, she didn't look Italian. Her tanned skin had more of a bronzed look than his; her strong, black brows weren't as thick but shaped thinner; and her nose, while long, was perfect. He didn't know what word he was looking for to describe her features until it popped in his head ... *Sculpted*.

Another thing Italian men couldn't help but notice were clothes. Her suit that consisted of a pencil skirt and a one-button black jacket might have suited her, but it didn't take him feeling the material in his hands to know it was probably picked off a department store rack.

He began to wonder how she would look in a tailor-made suit with expensive Italian fabrics, like he wore ...

Quickly folding up her jacket, he placed it between them on the seat as he slid over abruptly and put his face forward.

NADIA DIDN'T KNOW WHAT HAD HAPPENED. SHE WAS simply counting down from ten in her head, trying not to pass out, when she felt the cold chill of Dante's eyes on her. The moment she turned to look at him, his almost kind demeanor from when he had helped her get out of her jacket had quickly dissipated to a cold shoulder that matched his eyes.

She wasn't sure if it was the coldness from him or taking her jacket off that had instantly cooled her enough to focus on the situation at hand. With the fear of passing out finally subsiding, she went for her phone but couldn't find her purse. It must've dropped outside the car when Dante had thrown her in.

Shit. She couldn't even check how Haley had managed the meeting with Desmond Beck. *I bet she wants to kill me right about now ...*

The help Haley was banking on clearly wasn't going to happen.

Nadia wasn't sure if Haley was going to even believe her excuse.

Taking a side glance over at Dante, she thought, *He might be hotter than Al Pacino, but he's clearly as dangerous as Tony Montana*, as she was thrown into full-fledged *Scarface*. There was no longer any doubt in her mind because, *SPOILER ALERT ... the rumors about Dante Caruso are true.*

Thank God Haley hadn't chosen Dante's folder. She managed to find some relief in the situation. Then, looking heavenward, she made a silent wish.

I sure hope Haley had a better meeting than me ...

WELL, YOU DO TODAY, MS. BROOKS

"I say you should continue on with the vacation, sir," Amo told him, still behind the wheel and heading to their destination. "Getting on that yacht is the safest thing you could do right now. One-Shot won't be able to touch you in the middle of the ocean, and you seem to be his only target at the moment."

His soldier might have a point, but Dante hated running away. He felt like a coward and was about to tell him to head back to the casino hotel when he got a glimpse of his son's profile.

Leo hadn't shown much care about anything lately, but when he mentioned going on vacation on the yacht, he had seen a glimmer of interest cross his face. He knew his son desperately needed to get away from the city for a bit and couldn't take that away. Not when he felt his last child slipping from his grasp, like the rest of his children already had.

Dante moved his eyes from his son to the rearview mirror and firmly nodded.

∞

"You can let me out anytime," Nadia reminded them that she was still here. "Here's fine," she added, trying not to sound worried when she didn't get a response.

"I'm sorry you were dragged into this,"—Dante was the one to break the news to her—"but I can't do that in good conscience, Ms. Brooks."

Whipping her head toward him, she stared at him in confusion while the slight twang of fear returned to her spine. "Excuse me?"

"I'm afraid One-Shot might not take you as just an acquaintance now," he told her, reminding her that he had cared enough to get her out of Dodge. "You'll be safer accompanying us this weekend."

A short laugh escaped her, thinking he must seriously be fucking joking, but then she suddenly stopped. "No."

Hell no.

Absolutely not.

Nope!

Her little run-in with the mafia had lasted long enough, as far as she was concerned.

Cold eyes pierced into her soul. "I wasn't asking, Ms. Brooks."

Nadia didn't know what kind of women Dante usually hung around, but she assumed they were about as submissive as his men were to him. That was not her.

"Neither was I, Mr. Caruso."

Dante's brows furrowed at her response. Getting his way with her, unfortunately, wasn't going to be as easy as it usually was.

"If I let you out of this car and One-Shot gets even a whiff of who you are, he will find you and either kill you point blank ... or worse."

Nadia slightly gulped, wondering what could possibly be worse than that.

"He will use you to get to me." His brows relaxed their furrow, his eyes becoming slightly softer. "Since I got you into this mess, you are now the responsibility of the Carusos ... until I can get you out." Suddenly, his fierceness returned. "But I will not let you risk the life of my family because you do not want to go on a yacht for a few days. Got it?"

As much as Nadia wanted to shove her foot up his ass, she nodded ... *For now.*

She hadn't been more grateful for a car to come to a complete stop when the mad driver put the shifter in park. The eager teen was the first one to jump out of the car. Nadia, on the other hand, wasn't as eager for the next part of the journey to begin, not leaving the confines of the car until several minutes after the others.

Fuck. She should have never stepped out of the car, seeing exactly where they were. Nadia had been so busy trying to think of a plan to escape that she hadn't paid attention until she was staring straight at a white private jet.

It didn't take Dante long to notice something was wrong. "Everything all right, Ms. Brooks?"

She watched the back of his son disappear into the jet, unable to put her words into a sentence that didn't make her sound like a child in front of him.

The left side of his mouth tugged up, catching on. "You don't like flying, do you?"

"Correction," she began to clarify. "I *do not* fly." She left out the bit where she believed flying airplanes was like magic.

There wasn't an ounce of pity on his face when he spoke. "Well, you do today, Ms. Brooks." Dante then gave a brief nod to his bodyguard before turning his back on her and heading toward the jet.

Her fear of sounding like a child came to fruition as she suddenly felt like the annoying kid of a rich son of a bitch who didn't have the time of day to parent. And, with Amo suddenly giving her a nudge to get moving, he might as well have been the mean-ass nanny.

"I'm going!" she snapped at the prick when he was about to push her forward again.

As she began to walk past him, she was able to see him head-on, which gave her a better view of him than she'd had in the back seat of the car. "Jesus, how old are you?" she asked incredulously, seeing that, while his frame was massive in stature, his face still had a youthfulness to it.

He gave her a suggestive wink, making her regret her words. "Old enough."

Nadia couldn't help putting him back into his place. "But are you old enough to drink?"

His smirk instantly disappeared as his eyes turned into vicious little slits. "Get going."

"I'll take that as a no," she commented with a smile, knowing he was practically a child compared to her. Well, at least she was certain she could definitely outsmart him on her escape plan. Unfortunately, though, as she headed toward her second death trap of the day, it wasn't going to be possible to escape here. She needed brawn, and Amo definitely beat her there.

Her ankles rattled in her heels as she walked up the steps to the jet, only able to step into the big machine because of the big idiot right behind her.

"Not there." He pushed her past the first seat that was facing backward and was the closest to the door, to the one that was facing it on the opposite side, in the middle of the plane. There was a mahogany table between the two facing chairs, but hers was right next to where Dante was already sitting, so when she took her seat in the white, luxurious leather recliner-like seat, there was only a small aisle separating them.

When Amo went to buckle her in, she slapped his hands away from her. "I'm not a child ..." *Like you.* She looked at him ruefully, knowing he knew her exact thought.

He flexed his jaw before taking the seat facing her.

Dante had simply watched their interaction curiously, clearly trying to figure out the context he had missed in the few minutes he had left them alone.

Reaching for the seat belt, she fumbled with it nervously as the jet's door was closed.

Maybe, just maybe, she thought, hoping there was a way off this plane.

"Did you know that private planes are nearly as deadly as cars?" she said loud enough so the whole plane could hear her.

"That's not true," Amo retorted before looking over at Dante. "Is it?"

"Oh, it is," Nadia confirmed as she finally clicked her seat belt together before continuing, "Loads more people die flying private than commercial."

"You're lying. She's lying, right?" Amo asked, looking at his boss. You could practically see the nerves as he loosened the tie around his neck.

"Just Googled it." A younger voice came from behind them, one belonging to a face that must have been plastered to his phone. "She's not."

Amo was no longer loosening his tie. He ripped it off his neck.

Taking the slack from her seat belt, she gave it a good,

dramatic tug so it practically dug into her organs. "But, if you think about it, if something happens to your car, well, at least you have a chance of fixing it. Something goes wrong up there"—she pointed to the sky—"well, good luck fixing *that*." Letting the tip of her finger fall in a decrescendo, she whistled as if it was an airplane about to crash.

"Ms. Brooks," Dante called her name, as if in warning, while he reached over to cover her hand with his, "enough."

Nadia drifted her eyes to the strong hand over hers.

CLICK.

The sound of Amo's seatbelt finally clicking had her senses returning as she ripped her hand out of Dante's.

She gave the bodyguard in front of her one hellish look, now that he had killed any hopes of her getting off this plane.

It was worth a shot.

FUCKING FLORIDA

Nadia didn't know who was more grateful—she or Amo—when the plane finally touched the ground and slammed to a screeching halt. It actually might've been Amo, since he was the first to stand and leave the second the door was opened. She would be proud of herself for getting inside the Caruso's bodyguard's head if she weren't still in shock from doing the one thing she swore she would never do. She had still yet to even unbuckle her seat belt.

Again, the only thing she still saw of Dante's son was his back as he followed behind Amo.

"Are you coming?"

Nadia blinked a few times before looking at Dante, who was standing over her.

"Well?" His voice was as cold as his stance. She could practically see the agitation she was causing him by having to tag along.

"You know I don't want to be here, either. So, if I'm annoying you, remember that you only have yourself to blame for the situation *you* put me in," Nadia told him, point blank.

"I already apologized, Ms. Brooks, for the circumstances of why you are here, and I only ever offer my apologies once." He spoke as bluntly as she had. "And your presence wouldn't be half as annoying if you weren't trying to place your irrational fear on one of the last few good men I have left."

Nadia had figured that her constantly asking if the turbulence was normal when they had been up in the air was getting under Dante's skin, especially when Amo had finally taken over the job of asking.

It's not my fault the big ones are usually the biggest scaredy cats. The big buffoon's fear just happened to be the same as hers.

"If you'd like to stay on the plane, however, be my guest," he kindly offered from over his shoulder as he headed toward the exit.

Asshole.

THE WOMAN HAD ABOUT FIVE SECONDS TO GET HER ASS off the plane before he turned around and dragged her out.

Luckily for her, he heard the sound of the seat belt unclicking.

The small smile that played on his lips went unbeknownst even to him.

IT WAS DÉJÀ VU ALL OVER AGAIN WHEN SHE GOT INTO the back seat of another town car with Dante. Amo and Leo had already taken their places in the driver's and passenger's seats while the trunk was finally shut as the last of the suitcases was loaded by the small airport staff, just like it had been unloaded in Kansas City.

Long way from there now.

The sticky, muggy air that was practically suffocating her reminded her that she wasn't in Kansas City anymore. The bright city lights from the tall buildings were now replaced with palm trees, while the smog from the city was replaced with salty air. She could practically feel her slick, silky black hair rising from the humidity.

Florida, she huffed. The disdain for the state that wasn't hers could even be heard in her mind. Nadia had practically forgotten that getting on the airplane ended up in a completely different destination, and it hadn't been until the pilot had spoken the name of where they were landing, followed by the weather, that she'd remembered that fact.

"What?" Dante asked.

Nadia turned her head from the window. "Huh?"

"What did you say?" he repeated.

She realized her huffing "Florida" hadn't exactly been an internal thought.

"Oh ..." She trailed off, turning to look back out the window, staring at the homes that were different than the traditional homes she was used to. There wasn't a brick or stone in sight. Instead, most of the homes were covered in a mostly warm-toned stucco covering the Spanish-style homes. "Nothing."

Staring at her curiously, he slightly raised one of his dark brows. "Do you have a problem with Florida, Ms. Brooks?"

"No, it's not that." She lightly shook her head. It wasn't that she hated Florida, per se, or any other state, for that matter. She just didn't have any particular feelings about any place but the one she had called home for thirty years. "I've just never left Missouri before, is all."

You don't exactly put much thought into traveling when you grew up the way Nadia had. She had learned early on in life that dreams never came true while you were awake.

Dante looked at her inquisitively with his icy-blue eyes. "Never?"

She shook her head before shrugging. If she had wanted to leave Missouri, she could have done so by now, but she had decided to be honest with herself on why she hadn't.

"I love my city."

HE HAD TO AVERT HIS GAZE AWAY FROM THE WOMAN who was becoming mesmerizing to him.

I do, too.

But even his soul knew that was a lie now.

Well, I used to.

GRIPPING THE DOOR HANDLE, SHE COULD SEE HER fingertips turning white, knowing that her escape plan would be happening soon.

It wasn't her hand that opened the door, though, but Dante, who was now motioning for her to *come on* with his cold eyes alone.

She wondered why he was doing Amo's job until she began walking slowly down the dock. The Caruso body-guard was already on the yacht, seeming to be patting down the small staff, leaving Leo to take care of the bags.

Taking a quick glance over her shoulder as her cheap heels hit the wooden deck, she could see Dante only walking a few steps behind.

"Could you hand me that bag, please?" She heard the voice of the young man ask her.

She snapped her head forward to stare down at the black duffle bag at her feet. Bending her knees slightly, she quickly picked it up to hand it ov—

Oh my gosh. It took all of Nadia's might to keep from jumping in shock upon seeing Leo's face for the first time. The white gauze that covered his left eye sent a chill up her spine. She didn't want to know what it was hiding underneath.

Her mind instantly went back to, *"How many of your men has he taken out so far?"*

"A few," he admitted after a few passing moments. "And then some."

It seemed Nadia had finally found out what that cryptic "and then some" meant after all.

Swallowing, she snapped herself out of it, hoping her face hadn't given anything away. Nadia didn't want Leo to know she found his face shocking. Working with damaged teens was literally her job. It was what she prided herself on, and even after seeing all the vile and horrible things that they went through ... none of it prepared her to look upon him.

Nadia had what she called a gift. One look was all she needed to see beyond a child in pain in order to know their story. She had empathy for those who couldn't protect themselves because no one had been there for her, either, as a child. Not until she found Anna ...

Anna had had a gift like her, a gift that came as a blessing and a curse.

"Here you go." She pasted a smile on her face while she held the duffle bag over the water for him to take as he stood on the yacht.

His single blue eye, which was much different in color than his father's, dropped from her face sullenly to the bag she held out. "Thanks."

The pang that ran in her gut told her what she thought of herself before her mind even did. *Failure.*

She had just failed this kid, and that was going to be the last time she was ever going to see him, as she was about to make her escape. Nadia didn't know why, but she was sure that moment was going to be the one replaying in her mind until the day she died.

Leo Caruso was going to be the one that got away.

The disappointment in herself showed through as she watched him walk away. She couldn't believe she had been so wrong about him. So used to working with teens who had nothing, she hadn't gotten a chance to work with one who had every materialistic need.

She could feel the set of cold eyes on her now, and when Nadia looked over at Dante, she knew he had witnessed what had happened, and all her hopes of maybe playing off she hadn't been shocked at all vanished. Expecting a disappointed look on his father's face, much like herself, she didn't expect the sympathetic presence that held his features.

"After you, Ms. Brooks," he said with a wave toward the yacht.

"That's okay. You go firs—"

"*I insist.*" Any hint of sympathy was now gone. His voice held that demanding grip that was usually present as he placed a light hand on her shoulder before giving her a push forward.

Prick. It was, in fact, the father who was the rich asshole.

Being last to get on the boat wasn't in her escape plan. While she shakily got onto the boat, she also failed at trying not to seem like she struggled doing so.

The nerves in her belly began to stir as they started to undock and set sail. Dante staying one foot away from her at all times was going to make it tricky to escape if he didn't give her space.

Watching the dock begin to get smaller and smaller, she knew her window of opportunity was closing. It was now or never, if only this asshole would take one step away from he—

THE SUDDENNESS OF NADIA'S HAND BEING THROWN UP to cover her mouth had all three Caruso men looking at her as she ran to the edge of the boat.

"She's going to blow," Amo warned, and that was exactly why Dante didn't follow close behind her. He didn't need to see what she ate for breakfast.

Plus, they were so far out now that it wasn't like she was going to jum—

Splash!

"Holy fuck!" Amo shouted.

Leo looked around at them. "Did she just fall in?"

They quickly ran to where she had flipped over the ledge, with Dante leaning his head over the water. He didn't see her drowning. Nope, Nadia was trying to swim away.

"Well ..." he said, looking at his soldier, who was just staring down at her, "are you going to get her?"

"Hell no!" Amo told him truthfully. "I'm built like a boulder; I'll just sink."

Turning, he looked at his son, but Leo clearly wasn't eager, either, needing to only point at his nonexistent eye to say, *"Not it."*

"Goddammit!" he grumbled, throwing off his jacket. *What is the fucking point of having an army of men at my disposal for a time like this?*

"You've got time," Leo informed him nonchalantly as Dante quickly slipped off his Italian leather shoes. "She can barely doggy paddle and isn't getting very far."

Oh, how he desperately wished Lucca or Nero had come. Hell, he was sure his daughter, Maria, would have fucking jumped in, heels and all. Instead, he was stuck with these two.

Climbing onto the ledge, he took a single deep breath before expertly diving off. He cut through the water like a freshly sharpened knife cutting into paper before he rose back out of the depths. Shaking the water off his face, he adjusted his eyes to see that she, in fact, hadn't gotten far at all. Hell, he wasn't even sure you could call what she was doing a doggy paddle; that would be disrespectful toward canines who actually had the instincts to fucking swim.

Hearing a *plop* behind him had him looking to see that Amo had actually done something by throwing the life preserver over.

Dante had half a mind to let her ass drown right here and be done with her. Unfortunately, he found his arm hooking through the red and white ring to save the now-beginning-to-sink woman.

OKAY, MAYBE I DIDN'T THINK THIS THROUGH.

If the devil were on her shoulder right now, he'd be saying, *"Gee, you think?"*

Hitting the water had knocked all the breath out of her as she made herself fall like she had passed out instead of properly jumping off. But that certainly wasn't all, because she was certain she could swim as a kid.

All thoughts, however, were beginning to escape her, except for one, as water started to fill up her mouth and fatigue started to set in.

Fucking Florida!

She had taken one long dunk underwater, afraid this might be the end, when she felt a strong grip on her arm pulling her back up. Coughing up water from her lungs, she found her arms placed on something that floated, and she was able to put all her weight on it as she tried to catch her breath.

"Are you fucking crazy?" Dante's harsh voice cut through the end of her coughing fit. "You could have hit your head and killed yourself falling off the boat like that!"

"Well, I was trying to get away from you!" Her hoarse voice cracked as she yelled back at her rescuer, who was still holding her to the floating device.

"Yeah, well, you were doing a great job at that." His sarcastic tone couldn't be missed over the sound of the water lapping against them.

She tried to push her wet hair out of her face. "Well, I swam this far, didn't I? I wasn't expecting anyone to jump after me, let alone that person being a faster swimmer than me."

"Swimming?" He laughed sardonically. "Is that what you call what you were doing?"

"I went swimming as a kid once, and I thought I was going to be a much better performer than th—"

"*Once?*" He caught what she had said and seemed like he was reaching the end of his rope on dealing with her bullshit. "You've swam *once* in your whole life, and you still fucking jumped?"

She matched his tone. "Well, I decided to take my *fucking chances* with the water instead of *One-Shot!*"

It was like when she said the mysterious name, she could feel the mob boss' presence completely change.

He took a deep breath, his anger dissipating as he took his hand off her to push his own hair out of his face. "I suppose that was smartest thing you've done all day."

"Wow, thanks," she quipped, slightly wishing he had just let her drown if One-Shot was as horrible as he was making them out to be.

"Listen, Ms. Brooks"—Dante caught his own breath while giving her complete honesty—"if you're scared of One-Shot, like you should be, than the safest place you could be is on that boat for the weekend."

"Okay, fine." She finally gave in to him, defeated.

"So, we have a deal, then, Ms. Brooks?" This time, he removed his hand from the floaty instead of the one attached to his arm that held her to it.

She stared at the tanned hand, wondering if she should take the deal with the devil in the middle of the ocean or take her chances with the one out there … But, hell, this man had jumped in to save her, after all. She supposed she could give him a couple of days.

Finally, she took his hand. "We have a deal, Mr. Caruso. But, please, call me Nadia." There was no point in keeping up the pleasantries, as she had a feeling this was going to be the longest weekend of her life.

"Nadia," he repeated her name before asking her to do the same. "Dante, then."

"Dante," she agreed, their hands still clasped together, but she suddenly found her hand being dropped as he motioned for them to be pulled in.

"Just promise me one thing."

Nadia looked at him curiously, wondering what the hell he wanted now.

"Don't ever try to swim again."

DRAMATIC EFFECT THIS—

T he sound of water dripping on the deck could be heard from both her and Dante, from being drenching wet as they were finally pulled back onto the yacht.

"Have a nice swim?" Amo asked her with a smile.

Nadia shivered, too cold to get her smart comeback out before Leo's remark.

"I'm not sure you could call that swimming."

Just when she thought the youngest Caruso was nothing like his father ... "That would have been funny, if your father hadn't already made the same joke five minutes ago."

Both Leo and Amo furrowed their brows together as they looked over at Dante strangely.

She was just about to ask them why they were looking at him like that when Dante addressed the small staff that had just helped pull them out of the water.

"I'm sure one of you can show Nadia to her room and find her something dry?"

"Of course." A blonde woman in a white Polo stepped forward. "Please, follow me."

"Thanks," she muttered, falling in step behind her, but her steps weren't the only ones she could hear as she turned her head to see Dante following close behind, holding his dry jacket and shoes that he must've taken off before taking his dive.

"I'd like to get dry, too."

"Right," Nadia said with a nervous laughter. She tried not to feel guilty for his current state, but she certainly was responsible for him being wet.

Continuing to follow the staff woman, she led them to what appeared to be an outdoor living room with a bar that looked like an oasis in the middle of the ocean. However, it was when they went through the huge sliding glass door that her mouth dropped to the floor.

It was the most beautiful living area you could dream of, and it was on a freaking boat! Whenever Nadia thought of a yacht, she imagined them decorated in white and gold, but this was clearly no ordinary yacht. The walls were matte black, and the furniture was a rich velvet in a navy color. You'd think it would make the yacht appear too small, but it actually made it beautifully intimate, especially with the sliding glass doors open so you could hear the peaceful sound of the ocean. Nadia just wanted to be dry, curl up on the couch, and read one of her favorite books while she watched a movie on the ginormous TV screen. And that was just the living room.

There was also a small indoor bar and gaming section that held a pool table. This yacht was insane, and she couldn't begin to wrap her mind around not only the cost of something like this but the fact that it was just a "vacation home." She would be shocked if it was used more than five times a year.

This must've been the middle deck, as the woman led them to a staircase in the back. One half went upstairs, and the other half led down.

The woman motioned her hand toward a staircase that went upstairs. "Mr. Caruso."

Dante simply nodded his head as he started to disappear up the steps.

"Ms. Brooks, you may continue to follow me," the woman said as she began to descend below.

"Right, sorry." Nadia quickly fell back in step ... after she removed her gaze from the mob boss.

She didn't know what was upstairs exactly, but down below held extravagant cabins, and as they passed each room, she could see a suitcase sitting beside the foot of each bed.

Nadia's room came last. It appeared to be one of the more feminine rooms, decorated in a royal purple rather than a beautiful shade of blue. Unfortunately, her room didn't hold a suitcase that was going to be magically filled with her stuff from home.

"I believe we have plenty of clothes for you here, ma'am. We typically get a lot of late arrivals of the female variety." She winked before opening the small closet to reveal it jammed full of brightly colored clothing that appeared to be mostly skimpy dresses and cover-ups. "Boss likes us to keep anything that has been left behind." She tried not to chuckle. Then, getting a hold of herself, she pointed toward the chest. "You will find plenty of bathing suits there, and any other items you might need will be in the head." She now pointed toward a door. "Bathroom," she explained the boating term when Nadia seemed confused.

Nadia tried her best to give the woman a friendly smile. "Thank you ..."

"Lila."

"Thanks, Lila," she repeated the helpful woman's name. Then Lila finally left her to it with a smile.

Nadia headed to the "head" first, needing a nice, warm shower after today's events. First, she took off her jacket that had become plastered to her when she suddenly remembered ...

The check!

Pulling out the now extremely wet rectangle piece of paper, she carefully placed it on the counter. The ink had bled a little, but it was still legible, *right?* She would let it air dry and find out later. If it wasn't, she'd get Dante to write her another one. Hell, he might even add another zero after this disastrous meeting that had turned into a weekend.

She quickly undressed then showered in the small but luxurious bathroom before throwing on a bathrobe. She managed to find a blow dryer and a round brush to give herself her usual sleek blowout. It didn't take long until her shiny, black hair was placed perfectly in her long bob that barely grazed her shoulders.

Shockingly, there was even makeup, but she decided against her usual cat eyeliner and nude lipstick, only putting on a tinted SPF she found to protect her skin from the harsh Florida sun. She supposed the perfect business look she always displayed could take a break for a few days while she was forced to be here.

Finally leaving the bathroom, she headed toward the dreaded closet. She gingerly looked through the brightly colored clothes to find them all of the skimpy variety. Hell, she was better off wearing her robe than those.

Deciding there was no way in hell, she went to the

chest, praying for something that would cover her big ass around the man who had just given her a hundred thousand dollars for her charity, but when she opened the top drawer, then the next, then the next, she practically screamed when she opened the last.

Slamming the drawer closed, it was decided ...

She would stay in her fucking room all weekend.

DANTE SAT WITH HIS SON AND AMO IN THE OUTDOOR living area, catching the last few sunrays left in the day. They had all already changed into their vacation attire and had been resting, waiting for Nadia to join them. It wasn't until the sun was beginning to set that worry started to set in.

"I'm going to go check on Nadia."

"Good idea," Amo told him, picking up an hors d'oeuvre from the plate Lila held. "I thought I heard her scream."

"What?" Dante quickly got to his feet. "When?"

Amo plopped the little dish in his mouth. "When I went to go change."

"That was hours ago!" It was everything he could do not to slap Amo on his big-ass head. "And you didn't fucking think to check on her?"

"It wasn't like a screech of terror," Amo explained dumbly for him to calm down. "It was like one of those screams a girl makes when you get them white chocolate instead of dark chocolate when they're on their periods."

Leo, who looked like he might've been asleep, raised his sunglasses, revealing his bandaged eye underneath to give Amo a speculative look.

"Is that so?" Dante asked through gritted fucking teeth. It was no fucking wonder Amo was one of his last men who was still happily single.

"Yeah." He shrugged his big shoulder, clearly not reading the room. "You know they do it for ... dramatic effect."

Dramatic effect this—

"Ow!" Amo yelped, rubbing the back of his head where Dante had just slapped the shit out of him as he passed. "What did you fucking hit me for?"

"Don't be so dramatic," he told him from over his shoulder as he headed toward the stairs.

He saw the tug on his son's lips when he put his shades back down and went back to pretending to be asleep.

Fuck. He thought going on vacation was supposed to be relaxing. Instead, it was anything but. Now he had One-Shot finally targeting him, and what was worse was that now Nadia was involved. She wasn't meant to have been thrown into his shit. He regretted ever calling her back to give her the check. He should have just fucking mailed it to her, but his ego wanted him to do it in person.

He had made a mistake by letting his instincts throw Nadia into his car because now One-Shot could interpret it as him caring for her. Hell, she wasn't under-aged; he could just let her go and let One-Shot handle the rest, but his conscience wasn't letting him, and now he was playing babysitter.

At least, if he got her out of here alive, she was going to be easy to keep quiet. Handing money over to her little charity was going to serve as more than just a tax write-off now.

Finding her room was easy once he took the final step. It was the only door down here that was closed. Raising his knuckles, he gently raked them on the door. "Nadia?" he called out when she didn't answer.

He was just about to knock the door down when he heard a stir ...

Nadia cracked open the door to see a sliver of Dante's face on the other side. She couldn't help but notice his ice-blue gaze drift down to what he could see of her robe.

"Sorry, I didn't mean to disturb your sleep."

"I wasn't sleeping."

"You've been sitting in here this whole time?" He began to slightly narrow his eyes now, as his hand started to lightly push against the door. "Is something wrong?"

"Excuse me!" Nadia quickly lost the battle as he barged in. "This is my room!"

"Amo thought he heard a scream earlier," he said, giving the room a quick look around.

"I may or may not have screamed," she said, pulling her robe closer together. "But that was a while ago. A little too late now to be worried."

"Yeah, well, he didn't tell me till about a minute ago." Dante let his disappointment show clearly in his tone as he went to give the bathroom a check now. Returning to the bedroom, he asked the question she was hoping he wouldn't. "Why did you scream, then?"

"I was just being ..." Nadia couldn't think of the right word to describe why she had screamed after seeing the clothing options.

"Dramatic?" he asked with a raised brow.

"No"—*you freaking prick*—"silly." Yep, that was a much better word.

"Okay, then, what were you being *silly* about?"

Nadia went to open her mouth but couldn't think of what to say.

"I'll wait here all day 'til you tell me," he threatened, crossing his arms.

Clearly, there was no getting out of it. He wanted to know what caused her distress.

Shit, the crossing of his arms drew attention to what he was wearing now. Dante had changed into a looser white button-up shirt that revealed the top of his tanned chest. His black slacks were now a navy pair of ... *khakis?* No one in Kansas City would ever believe Dante Caruso would be on a yacht in *khakis*, yet here he stood, and Nadia had to admit the casual look made him appear somehow younger, fresher and, regretfully, even hotter.

When he was about to take a seat on the bed, she gave in to his relentlessness.

"Fine." She rolled her eyes with a sigh, heading over to open the closet door. "I didn't scream out of fear. I screamed in frustration because the only clothes available to me this weekend belong to"—she pulled out a yellow see-through dress—"Sherry"—she then revealed a red dress with the sides cut out—"Cherry"—now she headed toward the chest to open the forbidden drawer, grabbing a handful of string bikinis that she let rain back down into the chest—"and Missy!"

Stepping closer, he took a good look at the contents in the drawer. "This is why you've been locked in your room all day?"

Okay, when he said it that way, while he looked at her

like *that*, it did sound a bit dramatic … silly … or somewhere between both.

"They're just bathing suits, Nadia," Dante told her simply, like it wasn't a big deal. "We're in the middle of the ocean, for Christ's sake. Just try to chill out this weekend and enjoy yourself. You're safe here."

Unconsciously, Nadia took a deep breath, feeling relief wash over her almost immediately at his words.

"Plus, I promise you, no matter what clothes you wear, it'll be tough to break your"—Dante stared at her a moment, clearly thinking of the right word, until he did—"uptight façade."

Nadia's mouth practically dropped to the floor. "I am *so* not uptight."

"Really …?" Dante lifted his tanned fingers to the first fastened button of his shirt. "You sure about that?"

"What are you doing?" she quickly stammered out, taking a step back.

Smiling now, the mob boss finished unbuttoning his shirt, revealing his cotton white tank top that clung to his now apparent muscles underneath. Holding it out to her, his smile only grew wider. "Use this as a cover-up."

Nadia cleared her throat, both of them knowing she had just eaten her *I'm not uptight* words about as fast as they had come out. "Thank you," she said kindly, taking the shirt from his grasp.

"You're welcome," he said, clearing his own throat.

It was as if, just as soon as she had seen his ice-blue eyes become warmer, they turned freezing cold once more as his smile suddenly disappeared. She began to wonder what she had said or done to warrant the quick change in his demeanor.

Unfortunately, his voice went just as cold as he headed for the door, "I'll see you at dinner."

Staring at the door that had just been slammed shut, Nadia was simply dumbfounded.

And I'm the dramatic one?

Dante's jaw set in a fixed position as he left the room and went up the first flight of steps. He couldn't remember the last "kind" act he had given, and the fact that he just kept doing them with a woman whom he was beginning to find attractive, more and more by the second, made a weird feeling creep in his gut. Was it ... *guilt?*

Unfortunately, Amo and Leo had come into the inside living area. Even more unfortunate, they didn't miss a beat.

Amo was the one to ask the obvious. "What the hell happened to your shir—"

"Shut it," was all Dante said as he began climbing up the other steps to go put on another shirt. He knew how it looked, but he also knew it looked much worse than what had actually happened.

Right?

It was that fucking guilt that had him asking. Damn, he should have just let her stay in her room all fucking weekend. *Why did I have to go make sure she was all right?* It was all Amo's fault because he had said he had heard her scream.

What was even worse was the fact that Amo's idiotic comment had been right ...

And he thought Maria was fucking dramatic.

FATHER OF THE FUCKING YEAR

N adia had managed to find a black dress that had some length to it, thank God, and it actually covered her ass and the tops of her tall legs. The downside, however, was the top portion. The sweetheart neckline left nothing to the imagination when it came to her breasts. Thankfully, Dante's shirt fixed that.

Taking the white button-up, she slid it on, but instead of buttoning it, she tied it around her waist, giving the dress a more casual look ... while also expertly covering her goodies.

It didn't take long for her to notice his scent. She wasn't sure what exactly it was, but it smelled expensive and warm, with a touch of whiskey.

Shaking the thoughts of Dante's smell beginning to creep into her mind, she finally left her room. She was about as comfortable and covered up as she was going to get with the clothing options she had. *Uptight, pfft.*

Nadia wasn't uptight; she was just ... sensible. Plus, her being uptight was rich, coming from a man who expected you to ask how high when he told you to jump.

Heading upstairs for the first time, Nadia tried not to

feel self-conscious when she entered the room, but she couldn't help it when Amo and Leo both noticed the shirt was clearly Dante's. It appeared Amo seemed to be more amused than Leo, however, by the smirk on his face. Thankfully, Dante wasn't in sight—

Well, shit.

Hearing someone on the steps had her head turning to see Dante gracefully descending. Oh, how she wished she didn't find him so attractive, but he was quickly becoming her weakness.

When he simply walked by her without so much as a glance, she tried not to feel hurt. Why would she care if he looked at her, anyway?

Amo sat at the inside bar, unable to contain his smile. "Nice shir—"

Whack!

Dante smacked the back of his soldier's head, stopping Nadia from being able to hear what he was going to say.

"Oh, and he is *not* twenty-one," Dante told the male bartender, who had just poured whiskey into a crystal glass that sat in front of Amo.

When he watched his boss take the glass for himself, Amo frowned, his eyes immediately going to Nadia.

Nadia smirked maybe a bit too evilly at the big buffoon's clear embarrassment now that her suspicion of him not being old enough to drink had been proven. All young adults wanted to be was old enough to legally drink, and they didn't know yet that being able to buy your own alcohol wasn't as great as it seemed.

"Of course, sir. Sorry about that," the bartender, named Max, said as he lowered his head apologetically.

"And my son isn't old enough to drink, either," Dante warned in case Leo had any ideas, too.

Leo appeared unbothered and didn't seem like he was the least bit upset, like Amo had been.

She walked up to the bar. The smirk hadn't left her face as she stopped next to the sullen bodyguard. "I'll have a drink, however."

"What would you like?" Max asked from behind the bar.

"A glass of red wine would be fine, thank you." Nadia wasn't much of a drinker, but every now and then, she and Haley did enjoy a glass of wine with dinner.

You could practically hear the rolling of Amo's eyes as he swiveled on the chair and got up. "Shocker ..." he mumbled under his breath for only himself to hear. It was apparent he thought her drink choice matched her "uptight" persona.

"Would you like a particular—"

"Surprise me," she answered, cutting him off. The only thing she knew about wine was that she liked it, even if it came out of a box, and she wasn't about to embarrass herself pretending she knew anything about wine in front of Dante Caruso.

"Dinner's ready!" Lila announced.

Just in time.

Taking her freshly poured glass, she and the rest of them followed Lila to the outdoor dining area on the deck. The table was beautifully set, and the view was beyond breathtaking.

Nadia took her seat at the end of the table, opposite of Dante, while Leo and Amo took theirs on each side of her.

Their salad was brought out almost immediately. Nadia took one look at it and instantly knew this was going to be interesting. The dressing was green, and it took her two bites to figure out what it possibly was.

"What the hell kind of dressing is this?" Amo whispered under his breath so none of the staff could hear. He was still trying to swallow his first bite.

Leo had been smarter, taking a smaller bite, but it was clearly still just as difficult for him to swallow.

"Enjoying the salads?" Lila asked, dropping off fresh bread. "The avocado cilantro lime dressing is a chef favorite."

Amo went to open his mouth, but a kick from under the table, from Dante's direction, had him managing to fake a pleasant sounding, "*Mmhmm ...*"

It was all Nadia could manage to keep herself from laughing until Lila had left. "Eat some of the bottom with some bread. It's not covered in the dressing too badly."

Both boys immediately thought it was a good idea, as they each took a healthy piece of bread and cut to the bottom of their salads.

To be honest, Nadia could see even Dante was having trouble eating the top part of his salad, even though she was sure he wouldn't admit it.

Thankfully, their next dish was brought out quickly. When asked if they were still working on their salads, they followed Amo's suit of telling them to take it.

"Seared ahi tuna," Lila told them gleefully as she set a beautiful but rare-looking dish in front of her.

Amo's eyes went wide when his plate was set in front of him. "Oh, yum."

Again, it was hard for her not to laugh. She, however, wasted no time digging in. She was never going to be able to eat fancy food like this, prepared by a chef, on her budget.

"It's awfully ..." Amo had trouble swallowing yet again.

"Rare," Leo finished for him, the fish clearly not to his liking, either.

"That's what seared ahi tuna is." Dante was beginning

to get frustrated with them. Whatever tone it was, though, Nadia didn't like it.

"They're just kids," she told him, continuing on before Amo could get offended. "They just want pizza and fries, and I can't say I blame them after that dressing." Hell, she probably couldn't pay one of her kids back home to eat this food. "That lettuce didn't deserve that," she finished with a small joke to soften the possible blow from the fierce-looking man who was staring straight at her for speaking up.

She waited for his smart response, but then they all turned at Leo's light chuckle.

It was quite obvious to her that his father and friend were stunned. She wasn't sure why until she quickly realized she hadn't seen Leo crack much of a smile, let alone a laugh.

Leo was pretty quiet, and when he did speak, he didn't use many words to get his point across. He liked to blend into the background, not draw attention to himself. And it broke Nadia's heart because she knew exactly why he did that—his eye, or lack thereof. She was pretty sure that whatever had happened to him was quite fresh, considering his once white bandage grew muddier-looking in the center than the last time she had seen his face hours ago.

If there was one thing Nadia understood, it was the less you talked, the least attention you drew to yourself. Her friend, Haley, had perfected that.

She was at least thankful Leo's laugh had drawn Dante's attention, and it was as if his anger began to slowly dissipate.

"Here." Nadia scooped half her rice onto Leo's plate, and then the rest onto Amo's. It was actually really good and seasoned to perfection, but she didn't mind letting them have it instead. Finally, she took a piece of Leo's tuna and placed it on her plate, but as she did, she would have sworn his eye, that was as deep and blue as the ocean, had seemed mystified. Unsure what caused it, she knew not to draw attention to it as she then, riskily, went to take a piece of tuna off Amo's plate and managed to reach across the table to plop it onto Dante's.

Dante stared down at his plate, just as dumbfounded as the boys were that she had just done that.

"Go on," she spat after a few silent, awkward moments. "Eat up."

All three men picked their forks back up and ate.

She felt as if she was testing the waters, seeing what she could and couldn't get away with, with Dante, but she was almost certain it was the fact that Leo still held an almost hidden tilt to his lips that kept the big, bad mafioso silent.

"The rice is good," Amo practically groaned in thankfulness that there was something he liked.

"It is ..." Leo agreed quietly. "Thank you."

"You're welcome." She smiled over at the teen, suddenly grateful her attempted escape had been unsuccessful. Clearing her throat, she got her arising emotions under control. "Let's hope you two will at least like the dessert."

"Did someone say dessert!" Lila came back out, holding a pie.

Amo grumbled under his breath, "Oh Lord," but quickly ate his words when she set it down in front of them with some plates.

"Key lime pie!"

Nadia's mouth was already watering, "That looks wonderful. Thank you."

"You're welcome." Lila beamed, looking at her almost empty glass of wine. "Can I get you more wine?"

"No, thank you. I'm not much of a drinker." As soon as she said the words, she regretted them as the Caruso soldier rolled his eyes again.

"Of course, you're no—"

A kick from Dante's direction had him stopping his words.

This time, however, Amo looked at his boss fiercely. "*Ow*."

Playfully smirking, she hoped he had hit him in the same spot. She was pretty sure he had, as that one did appear to hurt.

"Would you care for a refill, Mr. Caruso?" Lila asked.

"Yes." He wasted no time handing her the now empty glass, clearly needing it.

Lila took his glass to the bartender and was back with it in a simple moment.

"Thank you." Dante didn't even let the glass hit the table, downing half of the brown liquid immediately.

Finishing up their main dishes, neither Leo nor Amo could stomach another piece of tuna, while Dante and Nadia enjoyed theirs. Not able to stand them struggling any longer, she took her last bite then pushed her plate off to the side.

Grabbing the pie from the middle of the table, she took a clean spoon to taste test it first. "It's good," she announced to them, who clearly did not trust the chef to replace a simple ingredient for a fancy one.

You could practically see the relief on Amo's face.

Taking the small plates, she cut a big helping of the key lime pie and handed it to Amo.

"Thanks," he said, digging in.

Cutting off another huge piece, she handed the plate

over to Leo with a sweet smile. Again, she swore his single deep blue eye became a little glossy.

"Thank you ..." The teenager took the plate politely. "Nadia."

"You're welcome," she said with a beam.

This time, she cut a perfect triangle piece that wasn't nearly as big and held it out to Dante across the table.

He stared at the pie critically, not taking it. "Why do I get a smaller piece?"

Nadia was the one to roll her eyes this time. *Men.*

Setting that piece down in front of her, she took the last dessert plate and cut another piece, this time bigger than hers but still not quite as big as Leo's and Amo's had been. And she did so smugly, out of spite. Handing this piece to him, she could see his eyes had drifted over to Amo's plate, noticing it was still smaller than his.

"Take it, or you won't get any," she warned him with an overly sweet tone.

Dante quickly took it while the boys' eyes had grown slightly larger, but they didn't dare say a single word.

That's right. See if I cut you a piece of damn pie again.

About to pick up her spoon to eat her own piece, she couldn't resist pissing the man off once more ...

DANTE WATCHED AS THE FIERCE WOMAN CUT WHAT was left of the pie in two.

She wouldn't.

His gut instinct was telling him that she wasn't going to do what she was about to do, but when he watched her place another piece on Leo's already empty dessert plate, his jaw began to set, because his suspicion, he was sure, was about to come true.

He did not mind the pieces that were going to his son. He found it *sweet*, actually, and it tugged at what he thought was his dead heart. However, when the last piece hit Amo's plate, his eyes turned into beady little slits at his soldier.

She would.

Why he fucking cared, Dante didn't fucking know. But what he did know was that he didn't fucking like it. Not one bit. And the fact that Amo seemed to enjoy being spoiled wasn't helping.

His hand itched to pick up his fork ... *and wipe that fucking smirk right off his—*

"Mmm ..." Nadia groaned, finally able to take a bite of her pie. "The chef might be better at baking than cooking."

Swallowing the bite of pie he had in his mouth was proving difficult. That small sound of satisfaction, along with the bit of cream she had just licked off her lips, made him have to adjust in his seat.

Dante took an inner deep breath and got himself under control. It had been a while since he had been with a woman. Every now and then, when he felt like he needed a release, he would take an out-of-towner up on their seductive attempts. But with his family, *the family*, and One-Shot being a constant problem in his life lately, the urge to fuck hadn't even entered his mind. He was sure if he had taken that blonde who had given him a wink at the bar in his casino hotel yesterday, he wouldn't find Nadia attractive in the least.

Not his dick, nor his brain, let himself believe that lie.

"I'll say," Amo agreed with her that he was a much better baker. "Do you cook, Nadia?"

What the fuck? His soldier had been trying his best to get on her nerves, and now he was easily being won by her cutting him a piece of fucking pie.

Suddenly, Dante's hand itched to pick up his fork again …

NADIA TRIED HER BEST NOT TO LAUGH. "IF YOU COUNT microwaving and ordering takeout as being a cook, then I'm a pro." Unfortunately for her, there were no passed-down recipes, let alone a hot meal prepared by a parent. Of course, it was no excuse, since she was now an adult and there were plenty of delicious recipes plastered all over the Internet, but her life pretty much revolved around her work, and she always thought her time would be much better spent on other things than learning to cook. "How about you?"

Amo shrugged. "Nah, I pretty much get all my food from the restaurants at the casino hotel."

Nadia looked at Leo now. Any chance she was going to get to learn about Leo, she would take it. "And who's the cook at your house? You or your father?" She highly doubted the latter.

"Neither," Leo said without a thought. "My older brother, Lucca, usually cooks, if he's home. He's a really good cook."

"He sounds lovely." She liked Lucca already.

All three stared blankly at her, making her feel like she was missing something.

Amo was the one to break the silence, but she wasn't sure if his words were serious or sarcastic. "He sure is."

Again, the awkward silence had Nadia moving on. "So,

do you live at the casino hotel or something, to eat all your meals there?"

Surprisingly, it was Dante who answered. "A lot of my soldiers have an apartment on the top floor."

Huh? Is he beginning to trust me?

Nadia was sure that information wasn't publicly known, yet he had trusted her enough to tell her. Why?

"That's generous," she commented. "And how long have you been living there?"

"Ever since I graduated high school and he gave me a *job*."

Even the way he said the word *job* told her what kind of work he did for Dante Caruso.

"And you?" Nadia asked, her eyes piercing the mob boss' young son. It might've been too late for Amo, but Leo was probably only halfway through high school. He still had a chance to not follow his father's footsteps. "Do you plan on working for your father?"

She could tell Dante was waiting on bated breath to know what was going to come out of Leo's mouth.

There was complete silence while Leo thought about his answer. Then he said, "I used to think so."

Only Nadia asked the one thing everyone else wanted to know. "And now?"

Leo drifted his one eye to the table. "And now I don't know."

Instantly, Nadia's heart sank, taking her stomach along with it. She knew his mind had only changed because of his eye. She desperately wanted to get to the bottom of his feelings, but with his father sitting on the other side of him, it wasn't the time nor her place.

That was a job for his fathe—

"I've had a long day." Dante wiped his mouth with his

napkin then tossed it down onto the plate in front of him. "Good night."

It was everything she could do to keep her jaw from hitting the floor as she watched him rise. But once he disappeared behind the sliding glass doors then up the steps, her jaw became practically sewn shut as her teeth clenched together in anger.

Father of the fucking year.

THE LINE WHERE THE OCEAN MET
THE SKY

Nadia woke up sometime in the middle of the night. She had always been a light sleeper, so when she heard a door opening, followed by footsteps padding down the hall, her curiosity had her getting out of bed and throwing on her robe.

As she passed the slightly ajar bedroom door, she instinctively knew which boy it probably belonged to and who was most likely still asleep, snoring on the other side of the other bedroom door.

Letting her feet take her to the bow, she followed her gut, heading to the front of the boat. It didn't take long to find the one who had snuck out of his room.

"Can't sleep?" she asked quietly over the ocean waves.

The back of the dirty blond hair just slightly shook. He hadn't needed to turn his head to know who it was.

Not taking a step, she stared at the silhouette of the boy in the night. "Do you mind if I sit with you?" It was always important to ask for permission to talk with a troubled teen. Forcing your way in to understand them would never work.

"Sure," he answered quietly.

Lightly stepping forward, she took a seat beside him on the deck of the boat, about a foot away from him. Nadia didn't look over at him just yet, let alone speak. They both sat there quietly for what seemed like an eternal moment as they watched the front of the yacht slowly cut through the sea. Sailing during the day was beautiful, but it was a whole different kind of beauty at night. Up above held the most beautiful night sky that was filled with a billion twinkling lights, while below, the now dark ocean sparkled back with every wave that broke the salted water. They went on forever like a perfect picture until the different yet mirroring views seemed to meet miles upon miles away.

Thinking back to when Dante had left the table, Nadia had wanted nothing more than to do what his father should have—comforted Leo. But before she could get a single word out, Leo had left the table, like his father had, leaving her with Amo.

They had followed to bed shortly after, retreating from the awkwardness of what had taken place, making Dante successful in ruining the night for everyone.

"So, your dad ... he's quite ... intense, huh?" she asked delicately, beginning to probe.

"You mean an asshole?" he said the word she clearly hadn't used. "Yeah, pretty much."

"Has he always been like that?"

"Yes and no." Sensing she didn't quite understand, he elaborated, "We always knew our father was an asshole, but he changed when our mother died."

Nadia had probably been in her early twenties when Dante's wife had died. Melissa Caruso's blood that had been splattered across the grocery store parking lot, along with the bullet casings, hadn't even been cleaned up when practically the whole city had found out about her gruesome death. No one had even needed to ask how or why she had been murdered. Everyone knew why ... because she had married the most dangerous man in all of Kansas City.

Even though at the time, Nadia had known nothing about Dante nor his crime family, but she had been smart enough to know he had enemies. She just couldn't believe she would get firsthand experience of the enemies he had attracted later in life.

"I'm sorry about your mother. I remember when it happened. All everyone ever said about her was how kind and beautiful she was."

Leo, who had his arms resting on his bent knees, hugged them a little bit closer to himself. "I don't have many memories left of her, but from what I remember, she really was."

It hurt her heart to think how young Leo must've been when she had been murdered, but before she could express that to him, he stopped her. It was as if she had popped a cork on a shaken-up champagne bottle; his thoughts began to just bubble out.

"Losing her was harder on my older siblings, since they had spent more time with her. My brother, Lucca, took it the worst out of us kids, I think."

All the things Nadia had heard about the oldest Caruso sibling had her intrigued to hopefully meet Lucca one day. She could only imagine how good of a person he must be.

"But, of course, none of us took it as hard as our father did." Leo's single blue eye hadn't moved from the ocean view, but he appeared to be seeing a different scene in his mind. "None of us lost as much as he did that day."

With her throat going dry at his words, she swallowed hard. *He changed*, she remembered the words Leo had just said moments ago.

Sensing her exact thoughts, he continued, "Dad was

always intense, but not with her. With her ... he was just happy. And I don't think he's been happy since." Leo's voice turned to a whisper. "Not even his own children make him happy anymore."

Nadia finally turned her head to look at Leo. From this angle, he looked perfect, untouched, but she knew what the other side held. Her heart absolutely shattered for the boy who was clearly lost at sea.

"It is never a child's job to make their parents happy. That was never yours, nor your siblings', responsibility. Happiness is something Dante needs to not only *find* but to accept all on his own."

She doubted the man who had almost everything couldn't find happiness after all these years. It was something the mob boss was no longer accepting into his life.

"Do you understand?" she asked seriously as she fiercely stared at the boy. She desperately wanted him to understand that not an ounce of his father's happiness ever rested on his shoulders. Hell, she didn't want Leo to blame any misfortune of his life on himself. "The life your father has chosen is his to make, and I'm sure your mother knew the risks as well. But you, Leo ... you haven't chosen this life."

Slowly, Leo turned his head as a single tear spilled down his perfect cheek. "I can't choose anything now. I'm stuck with this."

Her eyes drifted to the left side of his face. She didn't know what crept below that gauze, yet she knew it was as gruesome as the color of it now. His words might not have told her everything, but she understood enough.

"Don't think, for one second, that having only one eye will hold you back from the life you want. There are people out there who have done extraordinary things who have lost both."

Was Leo sighted? *Yes.* But would Leo ever look the same or be the same? *No.*

"That," she said fiercely, nodding her head to his lost eye, "is simply a scar of where you came from, and don't ever let that keep you from the life you deserve."

Wiping his cheek with the back of his knuckle, he went to wipe his other cheek, only to remember that not only would a tear not be there but could never cross that cheek again.

"How would you know?" he asked harshly under his breath. He appeared to be breaking.

Nadia took no offense, knowing he was lashing out in the only way he could. So, she calmly took a deep breath, looking at the line where the ocean met the sky. It was a reminder that, even if you came from two worlds, you could always find a place where they came together.

"I don't remember much of my mother, either. I just remember I loved her so much. Like your mom, she was so kind and beautiful ..." She let her eyes drift to the dark sky, looking at a particular star that sparkled brighter than the others. Knowing where the story was going didn't make it hurt any less, even after all these years. "She was murdered by my father when I was five, right before he took his own life."

Leo slightly turned his head to look back at her. His eye had lost all tears, and the deep blue orb had turned stormy ...

"It was a classic domestic abuse case," she told him, continuing. "But since their arguments were always about my mother loving me more than him, I blamed myself for my mother's death"—taking a moment, Nadia had to clear her throat for her confession—"for a long time."

It was apparent in Leo's intense eye that he was beginning to understand, as it was obvious he, too, wanted her to know that she couldn't blame herself for her parents' mistakes.

"I was put into the foster care system after that," she announced, her tone changing from something heartbreaking to somber, like this part of her life, while tragic, wasn't as horrific compared to losing her mother and being in a domestic violence home. "And with every bad home I was put into, I ran. While every good home I was placed in, I managed to ruin because I didn't believe I deserved happiness after what I had done."

"I'm sorry," Leo finally managed to say with a slight flex of his jaw.

"It's okay," she told him, letting him see she was now content with her past. "My social worker was overworked and frustrated, so she sent me to check out this charity that was just starting up when I was thirteen. And when I got there"—a smile finally touched Nadia's lips—"Anna took one look at me, and I swear she understood everything I had ever been through, right there." The brighter tone carried on in her story as she found her happy ending. "She got me into an amazing program where I got to go to a boarding school for free in St. Louis, and there I met my best friend, Haley. When I graduated, I came back to Kansas City and started working for Anna, because all I wanted was to help others like me."

"And now?" he asked curiously, wanting to hear the rest. "Do you still work for Anna?"

"Unfortunately, she passed away last year ... from cancer," she told him, letting him know that, while she had gotten a happy ending from her past, it didn't mean that there still weren't bumps in the road in the future. "But she left her charity, Moonbeam, to me, and I still get to help so many teens today." Proud of what she had accomplished was an understatement. Moonbeam, which had started out in the same building it was housed in today, was about to get an upgrade in their mission to help shelter even more at-risk teens, thanks to her and Haley. "That's why I'm stuck here." She laughed. "I met your father at his casino hotel for a meeting."

"Did you get your donation?" he asked with a slight smile, knowing why she must've come.

"Oh, I got a bit more than that," Nadia joked, looking at where she sat in the middle of the freaking ocean.

The two sat for a few more eternal moments under the moonlight, not needing to say another word. The hardest part had come, and now she had to wait, for not only when Leo was ready to talk, *but if.* It hurt to know he would have to come to her first, as all she had done was open the door.

Feeling like she had accomplished enough with Leo for one night, she stretched out the next few moments until she yawned then got to her feet. "What do you say to getting some sleep? That way, we can spend the day resting in the sun tomorrow?" she asked with a smile while she held out her hand to help him up.

"Sounds good," Leo told her after a few seconds before taking it. As he did so, both of them had a silent understanding that he was taking the helping hand not only literally but figuratively as well.

The walk back to the cabins below was spent silently between the two as they were careful to not wake anyone else on the boat. Whispering good night to the boy, she then opened the door to her room when she heard him speak.

"Nadia?"

Nadia turned her head to look at Leo, who stood down the hall just a bit outside of his door.

"Thank you." He said the words so gratefully that it almost broke her.

She swallowed, hoping her voice didn't come out hoarse from too much emotion. "You're welcome."

Watching him slip into his room, she slipped into her own and wiped away the tears that were able to fall upon both her cheeks. There was always that fear she had when she dealt with teens who had extreme cases ...

Nadia just hoped she wasn't too late.

Nadia felt groggy the next morning after going to sleep with tears in her eyes. She couldn't help but be affected by the teen. She hoped that at least while they were on the boat, she would be able to shoulder his pain for a few days.

Getting dressed for the day, she focused on de-puffing her eyes and followed up with the tinted SPF again. Quickly brushing through her short hair, she left the bathroom with a silent prayer that she would magically find something appropriate to wear.

Of course, she had no such luck.

Scavenging through the bathing suits, she didn't pay any attention to looks or color; all she focused on was which one had the most coverage. Finally, she came across a neon orange bathing suit that at least wasn't a string bikini. She had to admit, it did do a lot of favors for her, especially the bright color against her tanned skin.

She then found a pair of cutoff blue jean shorts that didn't cover much more than her bikini already did, but when she finished it off with the button-up shirt that Dante had let her borrow, she didn't feel so self-conscious. She looked perfectly appropriate to be dressed this way on a yacht and finally felt comfortable enough to leave her room.

You're going to enjoy yourself. It's not like you'll ever get to be on a freaking yacht again.

Mentally preparing herself for the day was important as she went up the steps. It didn't take her long to notice the glass doors were already opened once she had reached the landing. Following the sound of commotion, she saw Dante already at the breakfast table, drinking a coffee.

"Good morning."

"Morning." Dante had simply raised his eyes above his mug for only a second before instinctively looking back down then straight back up for a double-take to make sure he had seen what he had seen.

Thankfully for him, Nadia had been walking to her seat and didn't catch his action. He was simply noticing her slow change in appearance from her usual uptight self. He could still see that part of her, but now he could at least picture her having fun outside of an office.

Hell, after last night's dress and the orange bathing suit he could see peeking through under his shirt, he was starting to wish she had her clothes from home, too. It certainly didn't help that the shirt was his. It had been a long time since his shirt had been around a woman, and it was putting thoughts he definitely shouldn't be having about Nadia in his mind.

He needed to be careful about letting his gaze linger on her. He didn't want her to notice because, if she did, she might make a move, and he wasn't sure he was strong enough to turn her down right now.

Man, how he wished he had taken that blonde up before he'd left ...

It was everything Nadia could do to keep her eyes to herself as she took her seat across from him. He was wearing a casual outfit again with the top of his chest peeking through, and she just wished he didn't affect her, like she was clearly not affecting him. The mob boss hadn't so much as glanced at her since he had come into her room yesterday, and, honestly, now that she thought about it, she didn't know what she expected, as he had literally given the shirt off his back to cover her up.

If a man was giving you clothes to hide your body, it probably meant he didn't find you attractive.

Suddenly, she felt stupid for even caring about what she wore when she had come out of her room. She could be fucking naked, and she doubted the man would even notice.

"Would you like some coffee, Ms. Brooks?" Lila asked, holding a coffee pot.

"Yes, please," Nadia answered quickly, needing the pick-me-up ASAP after the events of yesterday, and last night on top of that.

"Didn't sleep well?" Dante asked, finally taking a proper look at her.

"You could say that," she told him, not wanting to reveal the reason for her lack of sleep.

Thanking the kind blonde, she poured some cream and a packet of sugar into her coffee that was sitting in the middle of the table.

The big sounding footsteps, followed by, "Mornin'," didn't require either of them to look up to know who it was.

A refreshed-looking Amo took his seat while Leo joined them, looking the exact opposite. Not even his sunglasses could hide his weariness, and his father took notice as he then danced his eyes between his son and Nadia, making her grow nervous. It would be fine if Dante found out she had a deep conversation with his son; she just instinctively knew Leo didn't prefer it, as most of their conversation revolved around Dante.

"Late night?" he asked his son suspiciously.

"Nah, he went to bed right after you," Amo surprisingly answered, getting Leo and her off the hook.

"Oh," Dante spoke, and it was like you could see his suspicion move from Leo to Amo. "So ... you two sat up late, then?"

Huh? Nadia didn't quite know what was hidden in his tone until a slow smile appeared on Amo's lips before he spoke.

"Why would it matter?"

Uh, no! "No, it was an early night for everyone." She made it extremely clear for them.

Did she just see a wash of relief pass Dante's face? He didn't *look* pleased with his soldier right now. In fact, it kind of looked like he wanted to kill him. But what did that mean ...? Could Dante have been jealous if she had sat talking with Amo all night?

Nadia practically laughed that idea off in her head. There was no way Dante Caruso gave a shit what she did as long as she stayed on this yacht.

"So, what's for breakfast?" Amo asked Lila when she poured him and Leo some coffee into their awaiting cups.

"Yogurt parfaits!" she announced before leaving to go

get them. As she brought them each a beautifully displayed serving, she could tell Amo didn't appreciate the beauty of them, due to their size. "You'll want to be sure to save your appetite for lunch. The chef is preparing something yummy."

"Great," Amo voiced, practically eating his parfait in one bite.

Leo had done the same. Except, as soon as he finished, he went to go lie down on one of the sun loungers. Amo actually followed behind him, only he had thrown his shirt off before lying in the sun, revealing that his shorts were actually swimming trunks underneath.

"May I borrow your phone?" she asked Dante before he could get up to do the same. "I really need to let my friend know I'm okay."

Not saying a word, he reached into his pocket then slid out his phone before giving it to her.

"Thanks." You could hear the surprise in her voice that he had actually done so. Nadia didn't know why, but she was afraid he would assume she would try to call the cops or something, saying he had "abducted" her. Again, it showed the trust they were gaining in each other.

She hit the ten-digit number, and the other end rang for a few moments before it went to voicemail. "Shit."

Dante lifted his cold gaze to her. "What's wrong?"

"Nothing," she muttered. "I'm sure she just thinks it's a spam call. Do you mind if I text her?"

"Go ahead."

It was hard not to be nosy as she went to the messaging app on his phone. She really freaking tried not to glance down at the preview they gave you for the previous messages, but her eyes instantly went to a particular message, due to the graphic Emojis that were used ...

THINKING OF YOU 🍃🍵

It was everything Nadia could do to keep the regurgitation from coming out of her mouth.

She had half a mind to text the poor woman back that Dante clearly didn't care enough about her to add her number in the contacts, but that would require Dante finding out she had done so. Hopefully, the woman would get a clue soon that even the Caruso mob boss was shockingly ... *just like all men*.

Sure not to look at any other messages after having her fill, she quickly punched in Haley's number and sent her a message.

LOST MY PHONE. USING SOMEONE ELSE'S TO TELL YOU I'M SAFE. SEE YOU MONDAY.

At least now, if she didn't see Haley on Monday, she would call the cops and come looking for her, and that gave Nadia relief enough to enjoy the rest of her weekend.

"Thanks," she told him, handing back his phone while trying to still get that godforsaken text message out of her head, along with the bad taste out of her mouth. "Are there any books here?" Knowing she wasn't going to be able to sleep in the sun all weekend, she itched to read one.

"There are some books under the television," Lila was the one to tell her as she refilled Dante's cup.

Smiling in thanks, she headed for the console placed under the huge TV in the inside living room. On the side was an open bookcase, holding a few decorative items and even fewer books.

She had to crouch to her knees to read the spines and, as her finger went through the options, she quickly realized she wasn't going to find a book to her liking. They were all nonfiction, and Nadia preferred fiction. Her life had been enough of a shit show, so when she read, she preferred to escape.

On the last shelf, she noticed a hardcover that certainly stood out compared to the others. For one, it had a spicy couple on the front, while the other covers looked quite boring. Picking it up, she quickly glanced at the back, reading the synopsis. It was a romance that happened to take place in a motorcycle club, and that was definitely not fucking boring.

Nadia enjoyed a good romance, but they were usually historical ones, and, from the cover alone, she highly doubted they would be anything alike.

Deciding to take off the dust jacket to avoid any remarks at her book choice, she headed back out to the deck.

She took a lounger on the other side of an already sleeping Leo and dived right into the motorcycle world. Instantly, the one difference she noticed between historical and contemporary romance books was that they certainly didn't waste any time. In her historical books, it took practically the whole book until the couple did the deed, but in this book, she didn't even make it past the first chapter.

Going from a sweet romance to *this* was like being thrown into a proverbial sex dungeon. The main character called herself Sex Piston, and her group of biker bitches each had a nickname just as worthy. The men of the club, however, were much like men in the real world, except they actually voiced they were horny twenty-four seven. But for some reason, it was strangely endearing when it came out of a hot six-foot-one biker who wanted to fuck you in nothing but his cut.

Nadia couldn't believe how easy it was for men these days. All they needed to do was read one of these bad boys, and they would have a woman all figured out. If only they knew the secret to all women was held within the pages of a romance book ... *divorce rates would plummet.*

But just as she had that thought, Dante came over to the remaining lounger.

Nadia thought that keeping her eyes from reading Dante's text messages was hard, but it was impossible to keep her eyes on the cream pages in front of her.

Watching his fingers slowly travel down the front of his shirt had her belly somersaulting in anticipation. *Fucking hell.* The man gave the hero in the book she was reading a run for his money, and his nickname was Stud.

Dante was a certified D-A-D-D-Y, and she was sure, if he were in this book, Sex Piston would be screaming it. His olive complexion graced every inch of him, and there wasn't a single tan line to be seen. Honestly, Nadia didn't know where to look. The man had fucking abs, for Christ's sake, and in his forties! Between the abs, the salt-and-pepper hair, and the swim trunks, she didn't know if she was melting because of the sun or him at this point.

Even his *chest hair* had her reeling. *Oh God, but the shorts* ... had her going back for another peek from behind her book. They were a gray pair that hugged his tone body to perfection. They not only highlighted his abdominal muscles, but the muscles in his thighs that were on display due to his shorts being on the fitted side rather than the loose ones that men had worn when she had been growing up.

Stop it! She had to snap herself out of it. She blamed the damn book, even though she had been stuck reading the same sentence over and over again for the last five minutes.

At least her stance on one thing had changed—she was

certain Dante Caruso didn't need to pick up a romance novel to know what a woman wanted ...

"Drinks?" Max was overheard behind them before he appeared, holding a tray of extremely large, garnished beverages.

"What is it?" Nadia asked as she stared at them quizzically.

Amo took his drink that was being held out to him. "Who cares?"

"Rum runners." Max smiled now, handing one to a groggy Leo. "But don't worry; I made theirs virgin."

The huff from the bodyguard at the end was not missed.

"Yours, however, are not," the bartender said, holding one out to her.

"Oh, no, thank you. I'll pass." It was a bit too early in the morning for her. She much preferred her glass of wine for dinner.

"What a waste," Amo grumbled, not so much under his breath.

"You know what ..." Nadia shot an evil glare down to him. "I will have one."

Taking the huge glass, she took a big, spiteful sip from the straw and, as much as she wanted to rub it in his big face, she was actually taken aback by how good the frozen drink was. "That's delicious, Max."

"Thank you." He beamed, giving the last one to his boss.

Taking another sip from her drink, she sat back and dived back into her book. It was hard for her eyes to leave the pages, only doing so when Dante flipped himself in the lounger to tan a different side of his body. Having all her attention on one male in the real world was enough, so it really made her focus on the heroine called Sex Piston. She was everything Nadia wasn't, and the more she read about the biker bitch, the more she fell in love with her. She envied Sex Piston's confidence more than anything. Sex Piston wouldn't have screamed after finding those clothes Nadia had been left with. Hell, those clothes were probably from a woman named Sex Piston. But even though she showed off her body, she still demanded the same respect that would be given to a nun ... unless she was in the bedroom, then she definitely didn't want to be treated like a nun. Nadia was right there with her, however, because she definitely wouldn't want Dante to treat her like a nun.

Before she knew it, she was another chapter in when the straw that hadn't left her mouth had struggled to come up with more liquid while it made a gurgling sound.

As she set her empty glass down, her eyes caught Leo's sleeping face, and she could see his cheek turning a shade of pink.

Nadia quickly put her book down and went on a hunt for a bottle she had seen lying around somewhere. Finding it under the TV, she went back out to the boys.

"Wake up," she demanded the two, and when their sunglasses had raised with them waking, she tossed the bottle at the big one. "You need to put on some sunscreen."

"We're Italian." Amo shrugged, putting his shades back on. "We tan. We don't burn."

That logic almost hurt her brain. "Where the hell did you hear that?" she asked, dumbfounded. "The sun doesn't care what you are; it will still burn you and give you skin cancer if you stay out long enough. *Now, put it on.*"

"Damn." Amo picked up the bottle. "All right, then."

Her delivery might've been a little harsh after that rum runner, but at least she was getting them to do it.

Taking back her seat, she didn't pay them any attention as they started slathering themselves.

"Can you do my back?"

Nadia drifted her eyes over. "Me?"

"Yes, you," Amo said, like there wasn't anyone else around who was perfectly capable of doing it.

Dante could be heard stirring for the first time in a long time.

Her eyes merely went back to her page as she flipped to the next one. "No, Leo can."

"Hell no," Amo told her. "He ain't rubbing shit on my back."

Rolling her eyes heavenward, she put her book back down. The downfall of big dudes was they had to look hard at all times. "You know, real friends rub SPF onto each other's backs."

"No, I just don't trust him to miss my whole left side."

Nadia's mouth practically dropped at Amo's "one eye" joke, not knowing how to react in the silence until Leo did.

"Fair enough." Leo laughed. "I don't even trust you, and you have two."

Nadia felt comfortable enough to chuckle now as she took the bottle and squeezed out some of the contents. "Turn."

Another sound came from Dante's direction.

DANTE TURNED IN HIS LOUNGER, THE DEATH GLARE IN his icy eyes hidden behind his dark glasses.

However, he was sure his soldier still could not only see it but felt his warning glare.

He had two best friends, and Amo was one of his best

friend's son. But not even his father, Enzo, could protect Amo from the wrath he felt raging in his bones. Dante wanted to do more than slap the back of his big-ass head right now while he watched Nadia begin to rub the liquid onto his back. Never once had he been jealous of one of his soldiers ... but there was certainly a first for everything.

He hoped Amo was enjoying himself, because that was going to be the first and last time he was going to get Nadia's hands on him.

"Ah ... that's the spot—"

Whack!

"Make it weird, and you'll be left with Dante rubbing lotion onto your back all weekend," she reprimanded the six-foot-something soldier after doing exactly what Dante had wanted to do by smacking the back of his big-ass head. He only had one criticism ...

Hit harder next time.

Amo was still rubbing the back of his head. "Sorry, I won't do it again."

Clearly satisfied that he had gotten the message, Nadia went back to finishing up his back.

Dante, however, wasn't satisfied. At least not until her attention went to Leo. He carefully watched her look Leo over, and when she rubbed in a still white spot on his cheek that he had missed, he saw her frustration with herself.

"I should have had you two putting on SPF earlier. I'm so stupid." Nadia wasn't happy that Leo's cheeks had turned the slightest color of pink, placing the blame of them getting burnt onto herself, even though Leo was not only old enough to know to put it on himself, but also Dante, Leo's father, was sitting right there.

When Leo grabbed the back of his shirt and pulled it off

finally, he let the woman cover his back, and that was when Dante saw it.

Nadia had taken the same care in covering both of them, like a mother would have. Her touch on Amo was no different than Leo's, and suddenly, his jealousy turned into a feeling that again tugged at his heart.

It had been a long time since he had seen anyone mothering his son. His daughter, Maria, would do a motherly act every now and then, but this was obviously different to him. And with every kind act toward Leo, it made him see Nadia differently each time.

It was only the guilt that crept into his soul that reminded him to stay away from her.

Men like Dante didn't deserve happiness. Not when he had buried his wife six feet below.

Satisfied the boys wouldn't burn, Nadia took her spot back on the lounger with the bottle in hand.

"I'm going to go for a swim to cool off," Amo announced, which had Leo following.

"I'll come, too."

Watching the boys head to the back of the yacht, she could see Amo jump straight into the ocean, while Leo sat down to let his feet dangle in. She could tell he didn't want to get his bandage wet.

Returning to her task, she squeezed some of the lotion out and began to apply it liberally to her risen tanned leg.

Okay ... maybe he deserved happiness, at least for the weekend.

Careful that his shades were concealing his insistent staring, he watched the woman, who was becoming more beautiful by the second, apply lotion to her body. Her bronze tan glowed more with each swipe until her legs glistened in the sun.

Dante was sure the lower half of her body was his favorite, at least from what he had noticed. Her calves were toned, along with her thighs. On first glance, you'd think she was just on the thicker side, but you could actually see the muscle turn under her skin as she moved her leg to reach a different spot.

She had a true athletic build, with a generous ass to prove it, but when she slipped his white shirt off her shoulders to finally reveal her orange bikini top, he was no longer sure her bottom half was his favorite.

Her bronze skin continued glowing with each lather. She had merely turned enough to give him a glimpse of her breasts, and, while she was bottom heavy, they were a perfect handful that had him closing his eyes to dream about ...

Nadia tossed the bottle onto a sleeping Dante. "Put this on."

She was surprised to find that he didn't argue like Amo had but did as she said without so much as a word.

Picking her book back up wasn't enough to distract her from watching him, so she had to completely turn herself to the other side in order to concentrate on the words and not gawk at Dante.

"Would you mind?"

She looked back over her shoulder at his words, seeing that he held out the lotion.

"I can't reach my back."

Internally screaming at her predicament, she had to think, *What would Sex Piston do?* But she knew exactly what Sex Piston would do.

"S-Sure." She swallowed, gathering her composure as she put down her book. As she took a seat behind him on the lounger, Dante waited patiently.

Squeezing out the contents with shaking hands, Nadia bit her lip nervously. *Stop being stupid.* She had just applied lotion on Amo's and Leo's backs, and this was no different.

But staring at the expanse of his back told her it was much different, and it sure as hell felt different when her hand touched his skin. They had been just kids, whereas Dante Caruso was a man. A man who had her body aching since the moment she had lain eyes on him in his office, but she had just been too proud to admit it until she could no longer deny it.

Goose bumps prickled up her arms at the fact that she suddenly had free reign to touch his body, especially when she got to his strong shoulders. She knew that was definitely going to be her favorite part, which was why she saved it for last, and it certainly didn't disappoint.

When a wild thought caught her mind that would have been Sex Piston approved, Nadia hurriedly rubbed in the last bit that was still white, then she made it disappear quite roughly.

"Okay, done," she blurted awkwardly, wanting to desperately put space between them, but as she quickly stood, her hand was captured.

"You need some, too," he announced coolly, pulling her down in front of him, making her unable to protest.

Still, she tried. "Oh, I'm oka—"

"Don't be silly," he said, using her words against her as he kept her in place. "You can't make a big deal out of us using it to not do it yourself."

Nadia gulped. "O-Okay."

Christ, she thought, *applying it was hard, but just waiting for Dante to start is torture.* He seemed to be taking his job seriously, making her technique pale in comparison, even before he began touching her.

Rubbing the liquid between his palms, he warmed it up so when his hands did finally grace her skin, it was like warm oil being caressed into her skin, unlike the cold, thick mess she had rubbed into his.

To say it was like Heaven to be fondled over by Dante Caruso would be an understatement. The things he made her feel with his hands alone weren't going to get her into Heaven. He made her feel sinful, in every good way imaginable, and she never wanted this moment to end.

Actually, she was starting to get the impression he didn't want it to end, either, with the amount of time his hands spent coating her body. It far exceeded the amount of time he needed, and it was as if he was exploring. Every inch of her, he had taken special care, and when his fingers danced under her top strap and came dangerously close to the side of her breasts, she thought she was going to explode with pleasure. So much so that her lips parted.

When his hands then slid slowly to the other side, her back practically arched in anticipation ...

Unfortunately, the light footsteps couldn't be heard until they were right next to them.

"Sorry." Leo quickly noticed that he might be interrupting something. "I just needed some water."

DANTE PRACTICALLY SIGHED WHEN NADIA HURRIEDLY left his touch in embarrassment to go sit back down in her lounger.

He had really been enjoying himself, too. Regretfully, probably a little bit too much until his son arrived, and he didn't miss that fucking smirk Leo carried on his face, either, as he went to get a drink.

Fucking kids. They ruin everything.

"**D**o you think you can make me another one?"
Nadia asked when Max had shown back up to
take their empty glasses.

"Of course." Max smiled, proud with himself. "Another
rum runner coming up."

"Now, that's what I'm talking about," Amo cheered,
coming back from his swim. "Keep 'em coming."

Nadia laughed, proud of herself the more she loosened
up, and when her second drink came, it tasted better than
the first.

"Oh, I didn't ..." Dante stared at the rum runner that
was being held out to him and was going to deny it, probably for his usual brown liquor, but he ended up just taking
the drink. "Thanks."

Lunchtime came shortly after, when Lila showed up to
their loungers with sandwiches and fries. "Who's hungry?"

"Me!" Amo urged like none of them didn't already
know.

Lila started handing out plates. "Well, I thought you
guys might enjoy eating out here."

"Great idea," Nadia told her with a smile as she took her plate. She wasted no time plopping a fry into her mouth only for her to barely be able to contain her laughter so she could see the reactions she knew were about to ensue.

She watched them all take a big bite of their café-style chicken sandwiches first, and finally died of laughter when Amo ate a fry.

"What the fuck is that?" he yelled.

Nadia plopped another fry in her mouth. "Truffle."

"How the hell do you always know what's in it?" Amo asked in frustration.

"I went to a boarding school, and I ate a bunch of interesting food there."

Amo didn't look the least bit surprised, "Of course, you did."

Leo suddenly met her eyes, both of them sharing a knowing look. She could see the fact that he wanted to say something to Amo about his comment, but Nadia gave him a silent look not to.

She had never cared what people thought of her. Many people assumed she had been born with a silver spoon in her mouth, and if she had spent her life telling everyone she ever met that it had actually been plastic, Nadia would be exhausted.

However, her focus being on Leo made her miss the fact that Dante had noticed the strange exchange between her and his son.

Amo now looked on the verge of tears from hunger. "Now, why do they gotta ruin perfectly good fries with that shit?"

"It's how they make fries fancy," she told him, glad to move the conversation along.

"Fries are supposed to be fucking greasy, not fancy."

Amo shoved his sandwich into his mouth with defeat. His next words were almost unintelligible while he rolled his eyes. "Rich people."

"They can't be—" Leo took a fry to try. "Never mind."

Seeing Leo wince, Nadia was honestly beginning to agree. The food was good, but it would be even better if the chef had taken their preferences into account. They didn't have to add a special ingredient to everything just to "fancy" it up. Some foods—and yes, even greasy food—were perfect already.

"The fries are fine," Dante practically scolded them with a cold voice when he tried them. "It's simple. Eat them or don't."

"They're just hungry," Nadia spoke up. They couldn't help it if they weren't used to this food. "If they had one descent meal they like—"

"They're not starving."

Anger rising in her, she didn't like how he was making her feel, like she was being *dramatic* or something. He was the one who should fucking care—they were his family. Giving him a death glare, she showed him how dramatic she could be as she cut her chicken sandwich in half then proceeded to give one half to Leo before giving the other to Amo.

"Eat it," she said, not allowing them any possibility to protest.

Leo got the message and was really appreciative. "Thanks, Nadia."

"Yeah ..." Amo might've said the words to her, but he looked at Dante while he said them, "Thanks, Nadia."

Satisfied, she went back to her delicious drink and fries, propping up her book to continue reading while she did so.

"What are you reading over there?" Amo's mouth was

full when he talked.

"Oh." Nadia gulped down her drink, thinking quickly. "It's just a girlie book."

"So, a romance book." Amo winked, catching the drift.

If by romance, you mean erotic, then ... "Yep."

Slurping her drink brought up the gurgling sounds again since she had reached the end of her second drink.

"Would you like another?"

Seeing Max come out right on cue had to be a sign. "Yes, please."

DANTE STARED AT NADIA STRANGELY BEHIND HIS sunglasses as she downed her now *third* rum runner of the day. Clearly, he had judged the so-called "uptight" woman too hard.

Nadia had no fucking problem telling him off. Her ass was lucky he knew she had good intentions behind it, because she wanted to make sure Leo was happy. If that weren't the case, that ass would be swimming home.

Plus, there was no way she was that uptight with the way she was throwing back those drinks. Dante had had two of those suckers, and even he was beginning to feel them in the hot sun. Rum was one of those alcohols you had to be careful with. It was sneaky like that, and the way Max was pouring them, he doubted there was much else in the glass. Hell, he was shocked she hadn't gone out of the sun to take a nap, like Amo and Leo had.

That book must be good because, *how in the hell could she still read straight at this point?*

"WHAT ARE YOU READING?"

Those words, with his curious tone, told her she had just made a brutal mistake being too enthralled in her book. She hadn't noticed Dante had been staring at her when she busted out in laughter from what one of the biker bitches in her book had just said.

"Like I said, just some girlie—"

Trying to fight to keep the book in her hands made her lose concentration of what she was saying, but of course Dante had slid the book out of her hands a little too effortlessly, making her think she should slow down on the drinks.

"Sex Piston?" he said, half in shock and in laughter while he slid his eyes across the page to read a passage. "Is that really what the author named her?"

"Her nickname, yes," Nadia clarified, trying to take it back in sheer embarrassment, though, again, it wasn't hard for him to hold on to it. She was sort of just like an annoying fly while he began flipping the pages.

OH GOD.

She knew he had gotten to a good part when his eyes grew wide. "No wonder you've had your nose stuck in this book all day." Seeing how far she had read into the book, he couldn't resist another joke. "You've been busy."

She ripped it out of his hands finally. "It has a good story."

"Uh-huh." He looked at her just as sarcastically as the words he had to say. "I'm sure everyone who has read *Sex Piston* read it for the story."

Nadia couldn't help but let the chuckle escape her lips. He might have had a point, even though the story actually was good. "Well, you can't have a book called *Sex Piston* in your library and expect me not to choose it, when the only other options are autobiographies and how to invest money."

Dante opened his mouth to tell her something, but she continued her rant, not letting him speak.

"And while I'm on the topic of things you could change around here ... you could let your chef know your kids don't like his food. That way, he could prepare them something different."

What he was going to say clearly flew out of his head, as it was apparent on his face that he had changed gears to address something else she had said. "Amo is not a child, nor is he my son. He's my soldier."

"I thought you called yourselves a '*family*'." As soon as she put her hands down from air quoting her last word, she regretted them.

Okay, now she was certain she'd had too much to drink.

Nervousness quickly grew in her stomach from the deafening silence, not knowing how he would take what she had said. Of course, it was apparent now that he was the boss of the mafia family. However, speaking it out loud was a different thing altogether. She had let her guard slip. Being on vacation with him had somehow made Dante Caruso seem less dangerous, but the man before her was extremely dangerous, and she needed to remember that. Actually, the whole Caruso family was extremely dangerous, apart from the two he had brought, Amo and Leo, who she was sure wouldn't harm a fly.

Kansas City was full of whispers about the family, especially with one member in particular whom they called *The Boogieman*. And whoever the hell he was, she hoped to never ever cross his fucking path.

Her words had struck Dante like an ice pick going straight into his gut.

I thought you called yourselves a 'family.'

It was true, they did. Every member had each other's back, like a brother, father, or son, depending on where you fell in the family hierarchy, but if he was honest with himself, it had been a long time since it had felt like a family. Then, to make matters worse, it had been even longer since he and his children, who were his own flesh and blood, had felt like family. Dante knew when he and his own children stopped feeling like a family, but he didn't know when *the family* had stopped feeling like one. He was sure they were synonymous with each other; it just took some catching up to do.

"I ... You're right," he finally said, coming up empty with what to say.

Nadia easily sensed the change in him, her tone becoming sympathetic. "It's okay. No harm done."

His mind instantly went to each one of his children he had recently wronged in order.

Nero.

Lucca.

Maria.

And now Leo.

The words seemed to shockingly slip right past his lips. "What if I have ...?"

Suddenly, Nadia caught on that they weren't simply talking about the chef's food with his bone-chilling voice.

"And now it's too late?" he finished the grave question.

Nadia let go of her book, reaching across to grab his hand. "I have *never* come across anything that couldn't be fixed with a *sorry* and some time."

Looking down at the soft, slender hand that covered his

brought the strongest comfort he had felt in years to his soul, along with her words.

She now spoke as if she was revealing the world's biggest fucking secret. "You just have to mean it."

THAT WAS OFTEN THE PART PEOPLE SEEMED TO FORGET. It was like it was foreign for people to actually mean their apologies.

It was simple. *You actually are sorry when you say sorry, or you don't fucking say it at all.* But even after all these years of human evolution, the concept had yet to be grasped.

When she felt the light squeeze on her hand as their fingers intertwined, all thoughts went out of her head as she was tugged in Dante's direction ...

DANTE COULDN'T BELIEVE IT HIMSELF AS HE PULLED the woman in for a kiss. It was possibly the rum runners, or the place, but it just felt right, while it was also indescribable. The peace that was beginning to wash over him while being with her, he was sure would envelope him when their lips met ... But, of course, it would all be too good to be true when light footsteps grew closer.

Leo cleared his throat to announce his arrival when he went back to his lounger. Dante had wanted to see his son happy again, even if it was just for the weekend, but he couldn't say he was exactly pleased at the shit-eating grin on his son's face.

Fucking kids. They were such cock blockers.

FOODGATE

Each one of them sat around the table, eyeing each other as they waited to see what Lila was going to put in front of them for dinner.

Nadia was certain Amo had made the sign of the cross, kissing his fingertips in a silent prayer for the food to be good.

When the salads showed up with another weird dressing combination, she went to take a sip of her rum runner to calm herself.

She didn't know why it was bothering her so much, but she was certain it was because it didn't bother Dante. All the unbearable man had to do was walk into the kitchen and tell *his* chef to prepare something different. Sure, Leo and Amo weren't starving, but Nadia understood what it was like to get fed food you didn't like, and *that* was probably why it bugged her so much.

A lot of her foster parents, the bad ones, either made her go without eating or never cared to ask what kind of foods she *had* liked; sometimes even forcing her to eat foods they knew she hated.

However, since she and Dante had spoken about it, she supposed she should give him a chance to fix it. Still, anger ate at her while she watched the two boys eat the bottom of their salads, so she sat there, taking her frustrations out on her drink as she sipped it dry.

Seeing Lila head toward them with plates, Nadia started her own prayer.

So help me, God, if this food is disg—

One look at the dishes that was being put down before them had every single one of their mouths dropping, including Dante's.

"Whole fried lionfish!" Lila announced proudly, on the chef's behalf.

Nadia was pretty fucking certain her food should not be staring back at her as the *thing* in front of her looked like a dead carcass served on a plate. Not even the lemon cut into a crown that the chef had placed on the terrifying fish made it appear a delight to eat. It only increased its jarring appearance.

Something in Amo had clearly broken, as he whispered, "I can't do it."

Oh, honey, neither can I.

She was giving Dante one final fucking chance, but he appeared to still be speechless as he continued to stare at the water monster.

Fuck it ...

DANTE STARED AT THE FRIGHTENING FISH THAT LOOKED like it had jumped straight from the ocean floor and onto his plate after being barbequed on the way up. Honest to God, he had never seen anything like it in his life. Of course, he had seen whole fried fish before, but certainly not like this. Lionfish had a different effect to see it ... well, *whole*. This fish either needed to stay deep, deep, deep down in the ocean where it belonged, or it needed to be served like fucking fish sticks. There was simply no in-between.

It was only when he heard a thump that he lost eye contact with the nightmarish fish.

Nadia had abruptly stood, causing her chair to fall backward at the movement.

"Lila, I'm sorry, but we will *not* be eating this tonight."

Everyone looked at her, stunned; the blonde woman even more so.

"Y-You won't—"

"No," she said with certainty, picking up the deadly plate. "Now, please help me take these back to the kitchen. I'd like to talk with the chef."

Oh no.

"Y-You would?" the blonde stammered, still stunned.

"Oh yes," Nadia said, picking up Leo's plate.

Oh shit. Not only had that been Dante's thought, but it was clearly the thought that went through Amo and Leo's minds, too.

Dante had half a mind to tell her *no* and attempt to calm her down, but he had seen enough women in his lifetime with the same determination in Nadia's eyes to know to stay out of it, especially when a woman had had a little bit too much to drink.

Leo gave his father a concerned look. "Should you do some—"

"Hell no," Amo stopped him. "They were foul to do that to the fish. Plus"—he got up excitedly, like he was about to go watch a show—"I gotta see this."

"Yep, we better go follow," Dante agreed, telling himself

he was only going to make sure it went okay, not because he was eager to see it play out.

Leo stood up just as quickly. "Sounds good."

The men swiftly caught up to Nadia, who walked like she was on a death march with those creepy-ass fish in both hands. All they could see was the back of her as she used her foot to kick open the kitchen doors with a thud.

"Where is it?" was all they could hear as they waited for the swinging door to not slap them in the face.

"Where is wha—" the chef's booming voice echoed in the kitchen then suddenly disappeared when he spun around. When he saw who it was, his tone came out kinder. "I'm sorry. Is there a problem with the fish?" he asked, noticing them back on his steel counter.

"Yes," Nadia confirmed the fucking obvious. "It still has eyes."

Amo blew a raspberry from his sudden laughter while Leo and he fought to look out of the right side of the kitchen door window. Dante had to laugh himself while he looked into the left.

"My lionfish is a delicacy," the chef explained offensively, looking at the plates. "You didn't even try it."

"No, we did not," Nadia said, moving to the fridge while Lila stood frozen. "Now, where is it?"

"Where is what?" the chef asked, appearing more offended by the second that she was going through his kitchen.

She didn't lose focus from her rummaging through the fridge. "The food the staff eats."

The chef held up a finger, like she had just said the most offensive thing to have ever been spoken in existence. "We eat what I prepare."

"I can't see!" Amo cried, fighting for Leo to move over.

Leo elbowed him in the stomach. "Well, I only got one eye, fucker, and your big-ass head is in the way."

Rolling his eyes, Dante grabbed the back of Amo's neck, moving him closer so his soldier could look through his window with him. It had solved his problem of being able to hear what was happening inside the kitchen, but the downside was his face was now plastered against Amo's so they could see out of the small window with one eye each.

Coming up empty with the fridge, Nadia took a deep breath. She faced the chef, and her frustrations disappeared when she tried a different approach. "Listen, you make wonderful food. Truly, you do ... but I got two kids here who really just want some chicken tenders or something like that."

"I am not a ki—Ow!" Amo huffed, holding his ribs where Dante had just elbowed him.

Nadia's sweet voice could melt butter now. "Please, I'm sure you have *something* they would like."

Maybe I should go in.

Dante could only see the back of the chef, and he wasn't sure how he was going to react to even Nadia's sweet tone. About to swing the door open, he stopped when Lila finally spoke up.

"I'll show you." Lila stepped forward in defeat. "Max and I have a stash in here."

The chef's jaw dropped to the floor. "Excuse me?"

"Sorry." Lila winced, heading to the walk-in freezer. She went in then came out with a big box that had been shoved into the corner that was labeled as *sauerkraut*.

You could see that Nadia no longer wanted to be in there when the chef went through the box and pulled out frozen nuggets and pizza.

"So, you've been eating this?" the chef asked then

suddenly gasped, "Have you two even been eating the dishes I've prepared for you?"

Lila winced again. "No, we've been tossing them in the bin when you weren't looking. Then we sneak in here in the middle of night to make us something to eat from the box."

It was like you could see the puzzle clicking into place on the chef's face. He had seen the signs, but he couldn't possibly believe anyone wouldn't like his food.

"Oh, mon dieu!" the chef cried, throwing the towel that was on his shoulder up into the air. He sputtered off some more words in French, but Dante, Leo, and Amo were too busy jumping out of the way as the chef flew open the kitchen doors.

Thankfully, he had been well past offended, so the chef didn't pay any attention to the three as he left for his room. They quickly went back to looking through the window.

NADIA STOOD THERE AWKWARDLY, PRACTICALLY waiting for the ground to swallow her whole. Not knowing what to say, only a long, "So ..." came out of her mouth.

"Would you like nuggets or pizza for dinner?" Lila asked, like nothing had happened.

"Pizza sounds great," Nadia said thankfully, with a smile, like the awkwardness had suddenly left the room. "Would you like some help?"

"Oh no," Lila told her. "I'll just heat them up really quick and bring them out when they're done."

Nadia didn't need to be told twice, grateful to leave the kitchen, as if it were the scene of a crime and she had been the murderer. "Okay, thanks!"

"Shit," Dante grumbled, letting his feet fly back to where he had come from.

"Run," Amo said with a harsh whisper, grabbing Leo's arm to get him moving.

It might've been bad that he had left his son behind, but it wasn't like Nadia would have killed Leo for watching. Him, on the other hand, he wasn't so sure ... And whether she would kill Amo, he doubted he could get so lucky.

Even though he might have been the oldest, he still beat them back to the table but was slightly out of breath.

He and a now exasperated Amo and Leo retook their seats, as if they had been sitting there all along.

What was that?

Swinging the kitchen doors open, she swore she not only heard but saw something flash a ways up. Thinking it must've been the chef, whom she had just embarrassed to death, she couldn't believe she had just singlehandedly started a foodgate on the yacht. She suspected there had to be *some* kind of food, other than what the chef was preparing, but she hadn't expected it to come out like *that*. She thought she had been planted into a fucking telenovela when Lila had walked out with that box.

Now, Nadia just hoped that any of the food they might eat for the rest of the weekend wouldn't have spit in it, thanks to her. She wouldn't blame anyone for it, because she probably deserved it.

Walking back to the table, she tried her best to keep a straight face, as if nothing had happened.

"How does pizza sound, guys ...?" Nadia trailed off the moment she saw their faces. "You saw that, didn't you ..."

The men shook their heads vigorously. They might've been smart enough to stay silent, but their ragged breathing had clearly given them away.

"Max!" Nadia called out, hoping he was near.

"Yes, Ms. Brooks," the bartender answered, as if he was Batman.

Well, there was one similarity between Batman and Max ... she hoped he would be able to save the fucking day.

"We're gonna need another round."

THE CONSEQUENCES OF TOO MANY
RUM RUNNERS

"I told you I don't want to," Leo frustratingly told Amo. They had moved into the indoor living area and bar while they waited for their pizzas, and Amo had been spending his time trying to persuade Leo to play pool with him.

"Why not?" Amo pleaded.

Annoyed, Leo finally gave the reason, "How the fuck do you expect me to shoot a ball in a hole? I can't do shit now."

Nadia's heart sank, along with everyone else's in the room. She had seen him struggle to do a few things, witnessed him try to stick pieces of food with his fork and miss. She imagined losing an eye would need time and physical therapy for your brain to rewire, but she could imagine even more just how hard it must be to go through.

Watching Amo sadly put the pool stick back down, she was absolutely gutted for the soldier, who looked guilty for even asking.

Nadia took a sip of her drink before getting up from the bar. Moving to the pool table, she picked up the stick and walked up to Leo, who was sitting on the velvet couch.

"I imagine trying to shoot a ball into a hole is the best practice you could do." With a tender smile, Nadia held out the pool stick to him. "What do you think?"

Leo stared at the outstretched stick while they all closely watched the one-eyed teen in silence for what he was going to do. It wasn't until he finally took it that the tension left the room.

"All right!" Amo boomed, rubbing his hands together and walking back to the pool table.

Neither Nadia nor Leo needed to say a word to each other. There was a silent understanding between the two as Leo went and started to play with Amo.

"Pizzas are here!" Lila announced, coming in with a pie in each hand.

The disappointment was obvious on Amo's face that he wasn't going to get to play pool after all.

Suddenly, Nadia was struck with an idea. Taking one of the pizzas from Lila, she took it over to a table by the pool table that was meant to hold drinks and set it down. "Why don't you two eat and play in here, and—"Nadia grabbed the other pizza—"we can enjoy ours on the deck? I like watching the sunset," she added, not wanting to miss it.

Amo and Leo liked the idea and agreed happily, while Dante agreed by taking their drinks to the table for them.

Nadia was surprised when Dante pulled the chair out for her. "Thank you," she said, taking her seat, only to be more shocked when he took the seat next to hers, since they usually sat at opposite ends, yet now he was mere inches away.

The beautiful setting sun only added to the proximity and feeling she was getting by sitting so close to the irresistible man.

Nadia should have been upset that she had been the

one to say something to the chef, as Dante had sat there stumped. However, she truly believed he had been so shocked to see his dinner staring back at him that he hadn't known how to respond. Whereas she did …

His response, or lack thereof, of the chaos she had ensued told her that Dante had agreed with her response.

At least somewhat.

Now, if he had disagreed with her request of wanting different food, she imagined they wouldn't be sitting here, watching the sunset together.

"Well, I have to say that this is far better than what we were going to eat," Dante said with a smile, picking up a slice of the cheap peperoni pizza.

"I think so, too." Nadia laughed, grabbing a slice of her own. "You don't think I was a bit over*dramatic*, do you?"

"Nah," Dante said, taking a swig of the brown liquor he had switched to. "Did you see that fucking thing? That chef dressed a fried lionfish with a crown. Now *that* was *dramatic*."

She died of laughter because it looked like the big, bad mafia boss would have nightmares over that lionfish. "Okay, 'cause I was worried you might hate me after that."

A confused Dante swallowed the bite he had in his mouth before speaking, "Why would you think that?"

The laughter suddenly eased out of her. "I don't know. Just thought you might've thought I was being rude."

"No," Dante said, easing her worry. "I know why you did it."

He does?

"You do?" she asked, surprised, before taking a bite of her pizza.

"To make Leo happy," he said simply before begrudgingly continuing, "*And Amo.*"

Smiling at the last part, she knew he cared for his soldier, but it obviously wasn't the same care he had for Leo.

"I appreciate you caring for him," Dante revealed quietly, needing to clear his throat to continue. "He's had a tough time lately, and none of us—I..." Dante changed his words, seeming to put responsibility on himself alone. "I don't know what to do to help him."

Nadia swallowed, carefully thinking about her next words, as she stared into those icy depths she could now see appeared a bit helpless. When it became too much, she averted her eyes and gazed at the low sun that had turned the ocean orange. "I think you bringing him here was actually a good start."

"You think so?"

"I do." She could practically see the relief starting to ease in his eyes. "Sometimes, kids just need someone who's not their parents, or even family, to talk to."

"Is that what you did ...? Talk to him?" he asked curiously, taking another sip of his drink. When Nadia's eyes went slightly wide, he came out with it, "I could tell you must've talked to him by the way he was looking at you. I can't get him to hardly look at me anymore, and you two seem to *understand each other*." He phrased the words with a slight hint of jealousy, but he wanted to make it clear. "I'm not upset, though. I'm glad he had someone to talk to."

Relief flooded her at seeing he was genuine. She had encountered how some foster parents didn't appreciate her talking with their children.

"We did," Nadia confirmed his suspicion, but she made it clear with her face that she wasn't going to divulge what they had discussed. That was between her, Leo, and the ocean. "We talked about a lot of things, but he didn't tell me how it happened ..."

It was a long shot to drop the last bit in, and maybe she should only want to hear it from Leo, as it was his story to tell, but a part of her couldn't help but want to know how it happened. Maybe if she knew, she would better understand him, if and when he came back to talk to her.

Dante sat back, the weight of the world apparent on his shoulders, while any ease that had been brought to his ice-blue gaze came flooding back.

"I'm sorry. I shouldn't have ask—"

"No, it's okay," he assured her before she could finish. "It's only natural to be curious about what happened."

Nadia sat there quietly as the sun ominously disappeared into the ocean, like it had been swallowed whole. The only thing they had been left with was the sound of the salted waves.

"One of my men went to pick up my children to take them to school," Dante began slowly, telling her the story, "and right before he was about to get in the car ... it blew up."

Nadia somehow knew in her bones the last few words he was about to say, but it didn't make them any less jarring as every single piece of her shattered into a million pieces.

"Thankfully, the blast didn't kill him, but he was unlucky enough for a fragment to lodge straight in his eye."

"Oh, my God," Nadia whispered, covering her mouth. The gruesome image that came to her mind, she was sure the real thing couldn't even compare to her imagination.

The fact that Leo still stood on this Earth brought tears to her eyes, knowing the initial blow didn't account for what came after. It was a testament to the teenager's strength for him to be where he was now.

But then it hit her. "It was ..."

"One-Shot," Dante said the name of the person responsible, a name she couldn't. "The last thing I want to do is scare you more than I'm sure you already are, but—"

"No. Thank you for telling me." She was grateful to know what had happened to the boy who had fascinated her all weekend. The part inside of her that desperately called to fix broken kids needed it. "I haven't slept from wondering what happened." It might've been worse than all the scenarios she had imagined, but at least the mystery was no more. Now she just might be able to sleep more peacefully tonight.

"Well, you should certainly sleep tonight," he said, nodding his head toward her almost empty rum runner. They had no idea what number she was on now.

She took a sip of her drink to finish it off, and the light change in mood brought happiness to both their faces. "If only I had a tub in my bathroom to take a hot bath, that would knock my ass right out."

"I have one in mine," Dante revealed. "You could use it, if you'd like."

"Oh no, that's ok—"

"Seriously." Deciding against persuading her since she was clearly hard-headed, he quickly stood up, taking her hand to come with him. "It's a waste up there with me. I've yet to use it."

"Really, that's okay," Nadia insisted, not wanting to intrude on his space.

"It's a clawfoot ..." he tempted.

"Well, why didn't you start with that?" Nadia said, practically breaking out into a run.

Suddenly, she stopped to quietly poke her head into the indoor area to see what Leo and Amo were doing.

"What are you—"

"Shh ..." Nadia covered his lips. "You know what they'll think if they see me going up there."

Dante wasn't getting why it mattered.

"And then I'll never hear the end of it for the rest of the weekend."

"You're right," he suddenly agreed, knowing Amo.

"I mean, it's not like anything's going to happen," Nadia stammered out nervously, feeling as if she was a teenager herself, telling a boy that he wasn't going to get to third base with her. "But you know how kids are."

"Yeah," Dante agreed again. "Of course."

Exactly. I'm just going to use his bathtub. Nadia didn't know why she was telling herself that. That was only something you had to do when you needed to convince yourself. And Nadia did *not* need to convince herself to not sleep with Dante Caruso. It would be really, really bad if she did ...

Right?

She saw the backs of the two boys still playing pool; it was now or never.

Yes, it would be completely irresponsible, she told herself while she and Dante made a run for the steps, hand in hand.

Right?

Holding on to the rail, Nadia followed Dante up the stairwell, feeling the consequences of too many rum runners finally start to catch up with her. At the top of the stairs, she toed her shoes off, afraid to walk on the white carpet. *Who the hell would put white carpet on a boat?* Gaping at the private lounge, she snapped her mouth closed when Dante turned to see what was keeping her when she didn't follow him through two open doors.

Making her feet move at the same time as she gazed around the lounge, Nadia nearly walked into a huge round chair piled high with black fuzzy pillows.

Dante frowned at her. "How many of those rum runners did you drink?"

Righting herself, she returned his frown. "How many drinks have you had today?"

"A few," he admitted.

Nadia gave him a superior smile, like the ones Haley would give her when she had overspent on a budget.

He went back to her. "Give me a number."

One, two ...

"I can't. I lost count."

"Same here."

Curiously, she stared at him, knowing that look. "You want to bop me, don't you?"

Dante regarded her, as if she had taken a swan dive off the balcony. "Excuse me?"

She drunkenly lowered her face to point to the back of her head. "You want to smack me the way you do Amo."

"Oh ... no." Dante's icy gaze sparked a small fire. "I don't want to smack you the way I do Amo."

Her rum runners kept her from recognizing his true meaning as it went right over her drunken head. "Good. I have to admit, I don't know what I would have done if you had taken me up on my offer." Moving around him, Nadia wished she had her phone so she could take a picture. The bed was a showstopper. The sleek black bed took up most of the room, which was twice the size of hers. Five people could sleep on it and still have space to roll over. "You must be a restless sleeper."

"Why?" Dante asked, giving her another strange expression at the personal question.

"The bed is the freaking size of Texas."

For the first time, he took his gaze off her to look at the bed. "You're exaggerating."

"Not by much. Where's the tub? In Oklahoma?" She laughed at her own joke, as if it was the funniest fucking thing ever told. She only stopped laughing when Dante hadn't even started.

Walking past the bed, he slid another door open.

Her eyes immediately lit up, eyeing the clawfoot tub glistening in the moonlight coming through the window it was sitting in front of.

Hell to the no. "I can't take a bath in that."

"Why not? I told you it was a clawfoot t—"

"Well, you failed to mention the giant window in front of it!"

Dante went to the tub and started the water. "Who can see? There isn't a deck below this room, and there aren't any ships close to us."

Moving to the window, she pressed her nose to the glass to see for herself. "Oh … Then you can leave. I can take it from here." She started untying the knot she had made to close the bottom of his shirt.

Instead of leaving, Dante opened a cabinet. "This is where the towels are. There are some soaps and bath salts you can use, if you want," he offered, watching her unbutton the shirt.

Practically salivating, Nadia had to check out the tempting items that could practically furnish a small bath store. Her attention wasn't diverted when he went to turn the water off.

"Rosemary lemon." Nadia winkled her nose, preferring not to smell like a Thanksgiving turkey, then moved on to Lavender Dream. "Got anything *other* than flowery scents?"

"You don't like flowery scents?"

"Nope. Makes me feel like I'm in a funeral home." Going on her tippy toes, she found a yellow bottle that interested her enough to grab it. "Got you."

"Which one did you pick?"

Did he stub his toe when she wasn't looking, because why was his voice sounding so hoarse? She held the now open bottle to her nose; it smelled like the perfect day in the sun, which was appropriate, considering where she was, but this somehow smelled better. It smelled of vanilla beaches and sea salt breezes, but the most intoxicating part of the scent was the sun-dried oranges. "Sunshine Kisses."

"Good choice."

"I thought so." She showed him the bottle. "It foams, too, so it's a win-win. Now, if you don't mind, I have a tub of warm water calling my name."

Dante reached past her to take two towels out then put them in something that resembled a clothes hamper.

"I didn't touch them. They aren't dirty."

"This is a towel warmer," Dante explained.

Nadia started to bend down to examine the contraption, but as she did, she felt a wave of dizziness attack her.

"Whoa ..." Grabbing the side of the tub to make the room stop spinning, she felt Dante grab her arm to steady her.

"Are you all right?"

"I'm fine. Nothing a few splashes of water won't fix. If you ever leave ..." she hinted.

"I'm going to watch a game in the lounge. If you need something, yell out, and no more rum runners for the rest of the night."

"Yes, Dad," she mocked then began to giggle when

Dante's face looked like it had been chiseled from stone. "You have problems with people joking around you?"

"Not when they are funny ..."

She laughed through blurry eyes. "Have any of your kids told you that you're a downer?"

"No." His face had finally moved, but only to frown even more.

Nadia, however, didn't hold back. "Take it from someone who has a best friend who is also one. You are."

"Then why are you friends with her?" he asked honestly.

"Haley asks me that all the time."

His honesty turned into curiosity. "So, what do you tell her?"

"That I don't pick and choose what I love about her. I love all of her." She spoke the words that came so simply to her. "Despite her lack of sense of humor."

"Are you and Haley a couple?"

"No." Nadia specifically blamed the last rum runner she'd had for the saucy wink she gave him. "I like men the way I liked my bath water—hot." Smashing a hand over her mouth, she almost tumbled backward into the bathwater. Luckily for her, Dante ran forward and held her upright.

"I don't think it's safe to leave you alone with a tub full of water."

Nadia gave him a *pfft*. "I would be fine if you quit distracting me."

"How am I distracting you?"

Unconsciously, Nadia splayed her hands over his chest while she noticed him trying to assess how drunk she was. "I'm s-o-b-e-r," she spelled the words out to him rather slowly.

"From where I'm standing, it doesn't seem that way to me."

The alcohol made her brave enough to keep saying the things she had been wanting to tell him. "You're just being overcritical of me, which you've been since you met me."

"I haven't been critical of you," he said, taking no offense.

"Ah ... Then it's your persona."

Okay ... now he was offended.

"What persona?"

"Condescending. You come across as being very condescending." Nadia shrugged, supposing it came with the job.

And now he was past offended.

"I do not."

She couldn't help but feel as if the tables had turned from when they were in her cabin and he was calling her dramatic. *Rightfully so.*

"You do. You're doing it now."

"Right now, I'm annoyed," he clarified the difference in a warning tone.

"Yeah, I get that from you, too. I was just being nice not to say so." She crossed her arms, the action causing her breasts to lift higher. "And if I'm annoying you so much, why don't you leave so I can take my bath?"

Dante took a cooling breath. "I'm not annoyed at you. I'm annoyed at myself, so it doesn't matter if I'm here or in the lounge."

She slowly dropped her arms back to her sides, taking in his sudden change. "Why are you annoyed at yourself?"

"Because, right now"—his next cooling breath came out rather shakily—"the only thing I can think about is you finishing unbuttoning my shirt."

"Um ..." Nadia licked her suddenly dry lips. "I wasn't expecting that."

Meeting her eyes, he gave a long pause for her to say something else. When she didn't, he turned to leave.

"Don't go." Nadia couldn't understand where her plea had come from, or why she reached out to grab his arm. "I must have hit my head when you pushed me into your car."

Turning back, he swept his gaze down at her again. "Why?"

"Because I don't know why I said that," she lied, knowing it was, but she couldn't keep her mind up with what her body was telling her.

"Want me to give you a clue?"

A thrill rushed up her spine when his fingers went to the top button of the shirt she was wearing. At the movement, his knuckles grazed her nipple behind the swim top underneath. Sucking in a deep breath, she waited breathlessly for him to give her another clue.

Cool air from the vent above raised goose bumps on her skin, or was it Dante's touch? With her heart racing, Nadia curled her fingers under the opening of his shirt. The firmness of his flesh sparked an arousal, which would normally mortify her that she was being so handsy with a man she had just met the day before.

Of course, Nadia was no virgin. At thirty years old, she had even experienced a one-night stand or two when the need had hit, but this felt like anything but. This felt like the start of a beautiful beginning or a disastrous ending. Which one it was, she wouldn't be sure until she was on the other side of it.

She had never felt anything like this with someone. The people whom she had dated or slept with, she couldn't say she had felt much for them. It was like all her emotions and feelings were reserved for the children at Moonbeam. But now, here on this yacht, with him, it was like they were all directed and focused on this man. Was it because she was far away from Kansas City and couldn't focus on the kids right now? Most importantly, was she brave enough to find out?

His masculine scent enticed her to say *yes*, as there was nothing soft or boyish about Dante. The musk he was putting off was pure, unadulterated, viral man that was as heady as three rum runners.

About to give in to temptation ... her hands slipped away, and she took a step back, pulling the plug on the attraction that was getting out of hand. "My water is getting cold."

Dante took a step back as well. "I'll lay out a clean shirt on the bed for you to wear. When you're ready to go back down, I'll be waiting in the lounge." He then left.

Removing her clothes, Nadia didn't bother to make him close the door. If Dante said he would stay in the lounge, then that was where he would be. Dante Caruso didn't need to stoop to being a Peeping Tom.

Sinking into the tub, she luxuriated in the silky feel. Letting her toes peek out of the water as she stretched out full-length in the clawfoot tub, Nadia felt the tension and arousal seep out into the calming water.

You almost made the worst decision of your life ... yay. She didn't know if her inner voice was congratulating herself or not. *A little taste wouldn't have hurt.*

"Who are you lying to?" she grumbled out softly, only for the world to hear. "You would let that man chew you up and spit you out ... and then thank him."

Goddamn, that sounds nice, she let her mind wonder at the thought of not having her head screwed on so tightly for one second. Then she remembered his face, how unbothered he was when she had turned him down after winding him up. It had been gentlemanly and respectful, of course, but oh, how she wished it were at least a little difficult for him to walk away from her. Like it had been for her to walk away from him.

The water had turned cold. She was about to stand up when something had her eyes going to the side to peer out of the huge window first.

"Oh, my fucking God!"

DANTE HAD SAT IN THE LOUNGE, STARING UP AT THE ceiling, trying to calm himself down. He had counted down from ten several times, only to start over because none of the pressure he felt building in his pants had eased.

Thank God she stopped us ...

He adjusted himself, taking another breath. *Yeah, right.*

Dante had to start over again.

Ten ...

Nine ...

Eig—

What the fuck!

Her screaming had Dante barging into the bathroom.

"WHAT'S WRONG?"

"That is what's wrong!" she screamed, pointing at a cruise liner starting to pass by with several cameras flashing.

She sunk lower into the water to cover her face. Her fucking ass would have already been back in Kansas if she didn't have to show the state of Florida her birthday suit in order to get the towel.

"Shit." Dante ran to grab the towel out of the warmer then stood in front of the window, giving it his back as he spread it out to block anyone from seeing her.

"Who's going to see you?" She didn't give it a thought that Dante's cold gaze had been on her when she had escaped from the chilly water to the warmth of the towel now wrapped around her. "Just a thousand people!"

"How was I supposed to know a cruise ship was going to pass?" he said, easily lifting her from the water. Carrying her into the bedroom, he shut the bathroom door closed.

She couldn't believe it when he stood her on her feet, and he was actually laughing now. "Oh, so that's what you find funny?"

He started trying to dry her off but couldn't help himself to laugh again. "Well ... yea—OW!"

Nadia had picked up one of the black fluffy pillows from the chair and whacked him with it ... gently, she was sure. "How does that feel?"

As she went for another one, Dante took a few steps back. "Now, wait a damn minu—"

Nadia had already sent the other outrageously plushy pillow through the air.

"Come on; I bet it just feels like a love pat compared to the ones you give Amo. Poor boy ..."

"Woman, you've lost it," he said, putting up a warning finger.

She waved the third pillow as if it were a missile in her hand. The flashing lights from all the cameras on the cruise ship that were taking pictures of her charged her need to launch it. "I suppose I'm just being a bit *dramatic*, huh?"

"That's it." Dante didn't give her time to let the pillow

soar as he came at her like a charging bull, making her wish she hadn't put that extra zing into the last throw.

Oh no. She tried making a run for it, but her efforts were fruitless as he wrapped his arms around her waist from behind.

Suddenly aware of the feeling of something poking into her back, she started squirming then stopped, tensing under him, realizing the towel had fallen to her feet. *Oh no ...*

Dante, however, had been highly aware of her nakedness as he spun her around at her hips to finally face him.

Her breath hitched, making her glance downward. She saw her breasts plastered against his hard chest, each heavy breath she took causing them to press deeper into him. The material of his shirt was damp where her body touched his.

Dante now looked down, too, to see what she was staring at. His powerful body tensed in unison at the sight.

Nadia was still trying to process what had just happened in the last few minutes to get her from the bathroom to here, now being swept up in his arms ...

"I should let you go," he said roughly, without making a move. The harsh tone in his voice hadn't come from a place of anger but a special place right between pleasure and pain.

Her chest fell deeper, the peaks of her nipples the only things resting against him for a single moment. "Is that what your inner voice is telling you?"

"No, it's my dick warning me."

"Oh ..." Nadia waited to listen for her own tightly wound-up head to speak up, but there was nothing but silence this time. Taking it as a go-ahead, she brought her arms up to wind around his neck, bringing her breasts closer to his chest than ever. "I have an idea. I won't listen to my head if you don't listen to yours."

Dante didn't need to know her head was being conspic-
uously silent ...

Picking her up, he placed her expertly down onto the
bed, without their skin separating for even a second.
"Woman, that's the most rational thing that has come out of
your mouth in the past ten minutes."

RESPECTABLE WOMAN

"**M**y name is Nadia."

Dante's brows rose upward. "I know your name."

"Just checking. You keep calling me *woman*. I just want to make sure you didn't forget my name."

Dante eased his weight slightly so he could get a better view of the perfect mounds of her breasts. "It's pretty safe to say I won't be forgetting you anytime soon. You screamed loud enough to raise the dead."

Nadia craned her neck to look over his shoulder. "The boys won't come barging in, will they?"

"Amo heard a scream from your room and then told me about it three hours later," he said, shaking his head. "What do you think?"

Dante didn't like the glint that entered Nadia's eyes at that piece of enlightenment. He had told her about it before, but now that she had come to know Amo better, it seemed to land a bit differently this time.

Feeling bad for the boy because of his reminder, he tried

to take her mind off whatever revenge Nadia was planning. The woman was lethal with a pillow ... and generally *problematic*, he thought after trying to find the word that best suited her. Unfortunately for Nadia, *problematic* fit. So far, in the time that he had known her, the woman was either too busy trying to solve problems, or she just caused more.

Seeking his own type of revenge, Dante covered her nipple with his mouth. *This is such a bad idea.* Nadia wasn't the type of woman he usually fucked with. He had never been attracted to women who lived in Kansas City. It didn't help that she didn't take his gruffness without giving a smart comeback, knocking him off the pedestal he had attained at being the top of the family organization.

But oh, how he wanted her—*nope, needed to fuck*—but even he was well past believing that. So, he blamed him wanting to fuck her on breaking his cardinal rule: You weren't supposed to mix alcohol. It led to bad decisions and regret, and right now, mixing whiskey with rum runners had led him here, between Nadia's voluptuous thighs. The want for her would disappear just like the alcohol in his system would tomorrow.

But tonight ... he thought as he grabbed her hips to adjust her the way he wanted with his dick riding the notch between her thighs, *I will give in to my drunken demands.*

Removing his shirt with quick hands, he settled down to business to arouse Nadia before she said something that would snuff out his raging hard-on. Stretching her thighs farther apart, he slid downward to go down on her.

Her hips arched at the first touch of his mouth. Licking the rose-red vulva, Dante didn't give her time to have second thoughts and started laving the sunshine-scented, damp pussy. Boldly, he thrust his tongue inside of her and started tongue-fucking her. He gripped her generous ass harder to hold her higher against his mouth. "Put your legs over my shoulders."

Her movements were slow, but her legs gradually climbed higher until Dante had her in the position he wanted. Nadia opened to every damn demand he gave her. Using his fingers, he stretched her open by small increments. The tight sheath was slowly opening wider as her arousal grew. If he fucked her the way he wanted, she would be hurting afterward. He made it a point to never leave a woman he fucked unsatisfied, but with a pleasurable memory when the night was over.

Gauging how aroused Nadia was by the rhythm her hips were keeping with the thrusts of his tongue as she started moving faster, Dante lifted his mouth and pulled her legs off his shoulders. Flipping her onto her front, he lifted her hips again until she was on her knees, begging as she pleaded for him to fuck her. It only made his dick somehow harder, causing him to press a firm hand onto her back and lowering her head to the bed, wanting her in the perfect position as his body moved between her thighs.

He obliged her pleas. With one shimmy of his hips, Dante pushed his cock inside of her welcoming pussy. Nadia might have lost her mind when the cruise ship had passed by while she was naked, but Dante lost his in the moment his dick impaled itself within her. His mind dissolved in a bliss he had never encountered before. Like a dandelion being blown into the wind, his mental capacity diminished until there weren't any cognitive abilities left. All that was left was the instinctual need to satisfy the lust-filled cravings she had raised in him. Not even with Melissa had he ever felt this all-consuming need that needed to be expelled or his body would explode into a million fragments.

She would lurch forward each time he would plunge inside of her, then she would thrust back on him, driving him higher inside of her.

"Careful. I don't want you hurting yourself," he grunted out.

"Why do men always overestimate their size? You might be big, but you aren't *that* big," she teased with ragged breath.

Dante couldn't help but chuckle at her snide comment. Placing a rough hand on her ass, he lifted it higher until he could feel it bouncing back against his abs. He groaned at the sight, coming to the conclusion that her ass was his favorite part of her body.

Deciding to return the favor, he covered her back with his chest so he could play with her clit. Dante started moving faster with each scream of pleasure she expelled into the pillow. His breaths went choppy, desire coiling tighter and tighter, as his balls smacked off her with each plunge. Grazing her back with his teeth, he felt the muscles in her pussy squeeze his cock tighter.

Giving a pleased murmur against her skin, Dante felt her trembling as her pussy started pulsating around him. He stroked the pad of his palm from the hand that hadn't left her backside over the globe of her ass, and felt his own climax take over, sending him rocking against her in a heated rush to come with her.

When they both stopped shaking, he rose to the end of the bed to cuff her ankle with his hand and slide her toward him.

"*Hmph.* What are you doing?"

Something I'll regret in the morning, I'm sure.

"I need a bath. You can keep me company."

"I'm not going back in there." She rose to her knees, trying to scramble away.

"Look around you. It's dark. I'll turn the light off so we can see, but no one will be able to look in and see what we're doing." When she didn't stop squirming, he tried a different approach. "Plus, what are the chances of *two* ships passing by us?"

Nadia didn't try to get away with that logic when he lifted her into his arms and carried her into the bathroom. When he placed her down, she stood motionless until a small flame flickered to life beside the feet of the tub.

"Exactly what are you planning, Mr. Caruso?"

Turning the water on, Dante stepped into the tub to sit down. He held out a hand to help her inside and waited until her ass was fitted snuggly in front of his balls to curl two palms over her breasts and pull her back to his chest.

"Making wine from sunshine."

The sun shining on her face had Nadia disoriented enough to open her eyes. She could barely manage the act, having to close them again as suddenly as she had opened them. She hadn't been able to see much, but she found it strange that the sun had been in her eyes. When she had awoken on the yacht yesterday, it had been dark, as the cabins were below deck ...

Wait a minute.

The sheets that hugged her felt different. She thought hers had been cotton, while these felt rather silky ...

Did they change my shee—

Oh no.

Nadia's eyes flew open with a quickness, fighting the

sleepiness. It was like it had worn off in an instant when she noticed she was definitely not in her cabin.

Images of a blissful, sexy dream of her and Dante flooded her mind. Only they hadn't been dreams ...

They had been real.

Oh God!

Her stomach sank to the pits of her own hell before she felt it rise back up. *Shit!*

Jumping up out of bed, she bolted to the bathroom, barely making it to the toilet when the contents of the many rum runners, along with last night's pizza, erupted.

It was like instant relief as she wiped her mouth on the back of her hand.

Sure she wasn't going to geyser again, she flushed the contents and got up from the rather cold floor—

Oh my God, I'm still fucking naked! Shit, shit, shit, shit! She really hoped Dante hadn't just witnessed her run butt-ass naked to go vomit in his bathroom.

Covering her front bits with her hands, she prayed to the one-night stand gods that Dante was still asleep when she poked her head around the corner. Nadia didn't care what kind of sense it made to cover her body, considering she was pretty fucking sure the man had seen more of her body than she had ever seen of herself in her lifetime, but she just expelled every bit of her liquid courage, and any bravery she had had just been flushed down the toilet. *Literally.*

Phew. She breathed out a heavy sigh of relief at seeing he was nowhere to be found. That made her lucky but also unlucky, considering how high the sun was up in the sky. She had no clue what time it was, and when she went down those steps for her walk of shame, in the same clothes she was now quickly dressing herself in from yesterday ... that meant that everyone on the ship might just be up to witness it.

Fuck. Nadia cursed herself for the millionth time when she left Dante's luxurious cabin. Her shaky legs didn't even want to start descending the stairs as she carefully listened for any signs of life that might be waiting at the bottom. Not hearing anything, she slowly took a step at a time until she was able to see that no one was in the indoor living area.

"Thank God. Maybe it is early—*Shit!*" Nadia bolted like her life depended on it, yet again seeing the backs of Leo's and Amo's heads on the other side of the sliding glass door. She was sure she might've seen Dante's face as he talked to them, but she didn't care if he had seen her or not. He had been a fucking accomplice. Of course, he knew she would have to take the walk of shame.

When she heard the sliding glass door open, she jumped down the last bit of steps to the lower floor that held the cabins. There were no words for the relief she felt once she closed the door behind her and was safely in her cabin, like she had been there all night. Nadia threw herself down on her made-up bed with a *thud*, and all the adrenaline that coursed through her veins to get her here unseen seemed to have evaporated. Hangover signs seemed to rush her all at once—the pounding headache, grogginess—

Oh no.

She wasn't sure how, but Nadia had to sprint to her own bathroom this time to relieve even more contents.

"Yep"—Nadia spat into the full toilet before flushing—"that should do it."

Lying back on the floor, she let the cool tiles try to soothe her.

I don't want to ever hear rum fucking anything ever again.

IT WAS A LONG TIME BEFORE NADIA NOT ONLY WAS able to physically pull herself together enough to leave her cabin but to also get the courage to look at Dante again with each unveiled memory that came back of last night.

"You might be big, but you aren't that big."

Yikes, that certainly was going to be awkward.

Remembering the feel of him inside of her, she was certain he actually had been big, but drunk Nadia wasn't about to stroke Dante's enormous ego. With her body practically melting at the memory, she got back to the point.

Usually, when you had a one-night stand with someone, you weren't going to be fucking stranded with them in the middle of the ocean the next day. She definitely didn't regret the hot and steamy session she'd had with Dante last night; she just wished she had thought it through enough to wait until *after* they came back from their weekend trip. That way, she could run back to her apartment and wait for him to text her, like every other respectable woman. Then again, rum runners didn't wait for you to return back to Kansas City to work their magic.

Messing up the bed for good measure, so it looked like she had slept in it last night, she pushed up the big-ass designer sunglasses she had found, hoping they would cover her sins from last night, and left her room.

She wondered what it was going to be like to face Dante. Unfortunately for her, she didn't have to wonder for too much longer as she was now facing him.

"You're alive," Amo noted with a smirk.

"I'm surprised I'm alive, too," she said, taking a seat at the table. She could see they must've just finished lunch. "Trust me."

Oh God. Focusing on the smirks now on Amo and especially Leo's, face, she knew that *they knew*.

Amo laughed, clearly taking in her appearance. "I'd stick to your little glass of wine at dinner from now on."

Phew. She breathed. *They only know about your massive hangover, so chill!*

Calmed, she was able to chuckle a bit. "I learned a hard lesson ... rum and I don't mix."

"Nadia! It's good to see you today!" Lila came out to greet her. "They just finished lunch. Would you like me to bring yours out?"

"Oh no." Nadia practically vomited at the thought. "I just need water, coffee, and some aspirin, please, if you have it."

Lila smiled in understanding before leaving to go get it.

"So, what did they fix you to eat today?" she asked them curiously, wanting to pull the attention off her raging hangover.

"You missed a good breakfast," Amo began. "Pancakes, sausage, toast ..."

Nadia, however, got lost in thought over what the soldier was saying when Dante abruptly stood from the table to go lie down on a sun lounger without a single word.

"... So, lunch was good, too." Amo's voice had trailed back just in time for him to finish.

"Th-That's good," Nadia commented, trying to place her attention back on the boys, but it was hard because she couldn't help but feel slightly hurt. *Is he ignoring me?* Her mind couldn't comprehend Dante would do that, considering they were forced together for another day or so. There was no way he was going to get away with that, so she clearly must just be overreacting. *Right?*

Seeing that Leo had noticed something about her, she pulled herself together to put on a smile. "I'm glad you two are enjoying yourselves now."

"Yeah," Leo said, his voice laced with a tone she didn't quite understand. He appeared kind of down, but before she could ask what was wrong, he got up like his father had.

Amo either didn't catch what Nadia had or chalked it up to Leo's normal behavior when he thanked her. "Yeah, thanks to you and those rum runn—"

"Oh God. Don't remind me." Nadia covered her mouth at the alcoholic beverage that must not be named, and it was like the bartender felt his senses tingling when Max showed up.

"Ms. Brooks, can I get you—"

"Nope!" Nadia violently shook her head. "You may not." She, however, didn't have the heart to tell him what she really wanted to ...

Never fucking again.

As far as alcohol went, she was now celibate ... and she was quickly about to find out that Dante was going to make her want to be forever celibate in another way, too.

The bastard didn't so much as glance her way after she finished her coffee and took the sun lounger next to his. The boys had asked her to apply sunscreen on their backs again, and when she handed the bottle to Dante to use, he told her simply, "No, thanks."

Frustratingly, Nadia had to even manage applying sunscreen to her own back.

He was perfectly fine with me touching him last night ... and him touching me! Or had he really? All those memories of last night, and she couldn't remember him kissing her once.

Last night had been all about *sex*, and that was it. And while she didn't complain in the moment, now that she was fully sober, she was able to notice what drunk Nadia hadn't. The small red flags that told her it would never, could ever happen again. While that would be fine, if the sex had been bad, it stung Nadia, because that had been the best night of her life, even drunk on rum runners. None of her sober sexcapades had come close to that one, and that was just sad ...

She couldn't believe the audacity of men. Once they had gotten their dick jerked, they went on to catch the next sucker. Heaven forbid they had to face the woman the day after and "acknowledge them," but that would require facing the consequences of your own actions, *and we all know men royally suck at that.*

With each passing hour he ignored her, Nadia couldn't even focus on the book she had yet to finish, reading the same cursed page over and over again. She couldn't believe women would even write this false crap. All women knew men couldn't be further from what was written in the pages of a romance book, yet they still succumbed to reading them, just to keep the hope alive that one day, they could find a man like Stud or whichever fictional character they were in love with.

Fuck hope. She slammed the book shut, having had enough. Maybe nonfiction was best. The real world might be cruel, but at least the stories weren't based on lies.

Like clockwork, Dante had come back from his swim, dripping wet in all his glory—

Stop it! She cursed herself for not finding the man repulsive for his behavior, while he continued it by lying back down in his sun lounger without a glance or word to her yet again.

Am I hideous or something? she asked herself, looking down at what she was wearing. Maybe he thought she was, and that was why he was acting that way. A lot of people wake up the next day next to someone who wasn't up to their standards if they had been sober. For Christ's sake, it was so common that they had a name for that—*coyote ugly.*

Shit, am I his coyote ugly?

Glancing over at where Dante lay still, she knew the asshole wasn't asleep, even though he was already pretending he was. Leo and Amo, however, were actually asleep, that she was certain about.

She studied the man, wishing she could find something, anything, about him that made him physically unattractive, yet she couldn't find a single fucking thing. She wished Dante Caruso were her coyote ugly, but the man was anything but. He was and probably would remain the most attractive person she had ever slept with, and that made her hate him just a little bit more.

I am the ugly one, Nadia thought, coming to the only conclusion left of why he must be treating her that way. He was embarrassed by the fact he had slept with her.

No! she stopped herself. Nadia herself knew she was not ugly and couldn't believe she was letting a man make her feel that she was. If he did find her unattractive, then fuck him.

I'll show you ugly.

Slowly, Nadia stood, removing the shirt Dante had given her and revealing the white triangle-top bikini underneath. Then, only when she was certain he was looking at her, did she leisurely remove her blue jean shorts. She adjusted the white string bottoms to sit higher up her waist, making sure Dante got an eyeful of her ass before she walked off. She remembered last night well enough to know where his hands had stayed firmly planted.

"Where are you going?"

So, he can speak ...

Looking back over her shoulder at the prick, she saw that he had pulled his sunglasses far down his nose to get an undistorted view ... *I guess he can see me, too.*

"Going for a dip. I'm hot." She decided to play it cool, like she didn't want to murder the asshole.

His brows furrowed together. "You can't swim."

"Says who?" Nadia said, walking off again. She didn't need his negative energy.

"You!" Nadia could not only hear the frustration in his voice, but she could see it in his face, too. "When you took a dive off the boat. Or have you already forgotten that I had to jump in to save your *ass*?"

The emphasis on his last word proved her theory right.

"Well, don't bother this time," she grumbled, giving the man the sight he wanted.

GODDAMMIT.

Dante weighed his options while he stared at Nadia's backside walking away. He could either listen to his head and go make sure she stayed alive himself, or he could listen to his *actual* head and get Amo to watch her.

The sight of her glorious ass made him not want to do the latter, but he found himself picking up the bottle of SPF on the ground and throwing it at his soldier to wake him up.

"What the—"

Amo shot up, prepared to fight, but quickly saw the bottle on top of him. "The fuck was that for?"

"Go make sure Nadia doesn't fucking drown herself," he spat at him grumpily, already regretting his decision.

"Why can't yo—"

Amo was already about to lie back in his lounger when he caught Nadia in her white bikini in the distance. "No problem."

It was everything Dante could do not to strangle his soldier when he practically jumped up to go watch Nadia. The only thing that kept him plastered to his lounger and his jaw tightly shut was the fact that Leo had woken up ... and was watching his every move.

Proud of herself, she smiled smugly as she walked to the swim platform at the back of the yacht. She sat down, dangling her feet into the warm salted water, feeling like she had beat him at his own game. Any moment, he would be comin—

"Didn't expect you to want to go swimming anytime soon," Amo joked, joining her.

Nadia looked back at Dante, who was already back to acting asleep on the lounger. Her eyes turned into beady little slits. *That motherfucker.* He had woken up his soldier to deal with her instead.

"I don't," Nadia huffed, dipping herself into the water just enough to wet her body. She pulled herself back out of the water just as quickly then walked off the way she had come, leaving Amo baffled.

Her excessively loud footsteps let her presence be known, and it took all her willpower not to flick him off when she sauntered by him in her wet white bikini. Knowing the sun was going to set soon, she didn't let herself dry off, heading back to her room instead.

She could practically feel his heated gaze on her backside this time, and now that she knew how to get his attention ...

He was going to pay.

THE KING OF KANSAS CITY

The look on Dante's face as Nadia joined them for dinner after disappearing made getting all dolled up for the last hour worth it. For the first time since he had given it to her, she had left his shirt behind to reveal her dress in all its glory. She had picked a sexy, red, ruched dress that hugged her body for dear life, as it was probably a size too small, but it really did a number for her curves. It was quite short, but she had checked her self-consciousness at the door, because this was payback, and her fiery-red dress with matching red lipstick gave her all the confidence she needed for retribution.

Her winged eyeliner was also back in action, along with her full face of makeup to prove to Dante that she was anything but ugly.

"Holy f—"

Amo's words came to a harsh halt when he was kicked under the table. "Wow, you look nice," he said in an unlike himself, gentlemanly manner.

"You look *very* nice," Leo corrected before turning to his

father and giving him a piece of his own medicine by kicking him under the table. "Doesn't she?"

"Ow!" Dante cleared his throat but was careful not to let his eyes linger. "Yes, you do."

Nadia might've felt a bit deflated on the inside, but she didn't dare let it be known on the outside. "Thanks," she said, only looking at Leo and Amo when she said it. "I figured, since it was our last night here, I should look nice for our final dinner."

"Good thinking." Amo got up quickly to pull her chair out. "Let me get that for you."

She gave the soldier the sweetest smile as she took her seat and he pushed her up to the table. This time, she looked at Dante, who was throwing ice picks with his icy eyes at his soldier, when she said, "Thank you."

At least the kids have fucking manners ...

"You're welcome," Amo cooed, taking back his seat but making his chair now sit a bit farther away from Dante. He had done so just in time for dinner to be served.

Lila brought out salads, but this time, they were dressed in a homemade buttermilk ranch, and the bread was delicious, like always. When Max came out, he brought Dante his usual whiskey in a crystal glass, and when he asked Nadia if she would like anything, she simply held up her hand and told him, "Too soon."

They were brought perfectly cooked filet mignons shortly after, with a healthy-sized, fully loaded baked potato and asparagus to match. The sight and smell made all their mouths water, and none of them waited to dig in.

"So, what do you do, Nadia?" Amo asked before taking a bite of his food.

∞

Dante's steak-filled fork froze on the way to his mouth. *Excuse me?*

Amo was one of his soldiers who didn't give a single fuck about anyone but himself. He was young and selfish, with an emphasis on selfish. That was why he and Amo got along lately—because he only cared about moving up in the family hierarchy and did his job well without worrying about a girl at home, like all his other men were at the moment.

Even Nadia was stunned by the sudden interest.

"I run a charity for at-risk teens."

"That's very generous of you."

He stabbed his steak with his fork. *I'll show you fucking generous.*

"You should come by Moonbeam"—Nadia sliced into her steak with a smile—"and volunteer sometime."

"Oh, that's okay." Amo shrugged. "I'm not the volunteer type."

That was certainly true about his soldier, at least.

Nadia laughed. "Volunteering is good for the soul."

"So is working for money," Amo told her unapologetically.

See? Selfish.

"Just stop by sometime to say hi, okay? I think you just might find a reason to come back."

Dante studied Nadia then. He could see by the sly look in her eyes that she had settled on a plan she had been searching for last night. He just didn't know what.

If Amo was smart, he wouldn't step a single foot inside her facility, because he knew that look ... but he certainly wasn't going to give his soldier a heads-up. He was going to take that as payback from having to watch his soldier hitting on Nadia all day.

If Amo didn't realize she saw him as a child, and a child only, he had a rude awakening coming. That was the only reason Dante could even stand watching his soldier make a fool of himself, because if one thing was proven last night, it was that Nadia preferred men ... older men.

"You should come, too." Nadia directed her attention to Leo now. "Stop by every now and then to say hi."

Leo merely nodded his head. "Sure."

Nadia sullenly went back to cutting another piece of her steak, and even Dante couldn't believe his son. Come to think of it, he noticed Leo hadn't been surprised one bit by the fact that Nadia ran a charity. Clearly, that was one of their topics of conversation when his son and Nadia had their little chat.

"Do you have any children?"

Nadia coughed. The abrupt question had sent a piece of food down the wrong way. "No," she managed to get out, clearing her throat.

"Really?" Amo asked, surprised. "Thought someone would have tried to tie you down by now."

Nadia had to talk over how loudly Dante was stabbing his steak with his fork. "No, it's not that. I just don't want children."

She had said it so nonchalantly, thinking nothing of it, because that was how she had always felt since the day she had been old enough to grasp how a child was born. It was nothing new to her, but she looked up, feeling conscious of the three of them strangely staring at her.

Amo was the one who was either brave or dumb enough

to say what they were all thinking. "But you'd be a great mom."

"Thank you." She appreciated his words, knowing they had come from a good place. It was a relatively new time for women to openly admit they didn't want to have children of their own, and while it was easier to tell people to mind their business, it was also beneficial to tell others your reasoning for deciding against bringing another life onto this Earth, especially when it came to kids she helped. She had promised herself long ago that, if they were curious about something, she would always answer their questions openly and honestly. "But there are plenty of children out there already who need me, and that is good enough for me."

And it truly was for Nadia. Her calling wasn't to be a mother. Her calling was to help those who didn't have one. The only mom she was planning to be was a dog one when she eventually moved out of the apartment.

She could see the understanding pass over Amo's expression. It was like he could truly see her now, and she knew he meant every one of his next words. "You're a really great person, Nad—"

"Could you stop blowing smoke up her ass just so you can sleep with her?" Dante hissed at his soldier coldly.

Everyone went deathly silent at his outburst.

Nadia, on the other hand, couldn't believe the man she had spent last night with had said that. She knew Amo hadn't said that last part to fuck her. He had said it because, unlike *him,* Amo was a good person deep down.

Wiping her mouth with her napkin, she felt pure fury rise in her veins. "Thank you, Amo." Her once sweet tone turned deadly harsh as she directed her next words to someone else. "I wish it took blowing smoke up my ass to get me into bed." Throwing her napkin down on her plate, she stood then walked off as her appetite and weekend had now been ruined.

It turned out that getting all dressed up hadn't been worth it at all.

OH GOD, DANTE HAD FUCKING REGRETTED THE WORDS the moment they had left his lips. When was he going to learn that you couldn't take back the things you did, let alone said?

He wasn't the king of Kansas City anymore. He was the king of ruining every relationship he had ever had or might ever have. Dante Caruso was the biggest piece of shit on the planet, and what did it say about him that he would agree?

Each step he took to his room made him feel guiltier, and even though he didn't take the stairs down to Nadia's, he knew there was going to be a bigger guilt waiting for him if he apologized.

Opening his door, he noticed the item that had been placed on his bed immediately. He knew what it was already, but it didn't make him hurt any less the closer he got to it until he saw what was lying on top.

His white button-up shirt that he had given Nadia had been perfectly folded, awaiting his return. He had given it to her on the first night, hoping it would make her feel secure and safe enough to leave her room, and it killed him to think it no longer provided that for her. That *he* no longer provided that for her.

He didn't know if it was the returning of his shirt or the rectangle piece of paper that had been torn into two that rested on top that hurt more. The one-hundred-thousand-dollar check that was now rendered useless had him feeling as if he himself had been ripped in half. He knew it that meant for her to do that. She had spoken about her charity and the children she helped like nothing else in her life mattered more than them. So, for her to choose to give up the money to help build her kids a new facility meant that he had gone a step too far.

I have never come across anything that couldn't be fixed with a 'sorry' and some time. Her words from yesterday came to his mind, but as he picked up the ripped-up check, he couldn't help but think that there was no amount of sorry or time that could fix this. Like he felt with everyone he wronged in his life lately, *some things aren't meant to be fixed.*

Dante picked up his shirt and brought it closer to his face. It smelled of detergent, as any trace of her had been washed away. He had secretly hoped it smelled of sunshine, wanting to remember ...

... Dante must've only slept an hour or two when his eyes drifted open. The only reason he knew that was because the sun had yet to rise, along with the pounding headache. Then he felt the sleeping figure next to him before he actually saw her.

Many times, he had fucked a woman after his wife's passing, but this time was different. For one, he had always taken the woman to her room in his hotel and was able to escape shortly after to walk the short distance back up to his penthouse to never have to see her again if he didn't want. That was why he preferred women who were just visiting the city. Here, with Nadia, there was nowhere for him to go. He not only let her into his bed, but he wasn't going to be able to escape her until they returned to Kansas City.

Secondly, he had never actually felt comfortable enough to fall asleep by his one-night stands. He had them for one reason, and one reason only—he sought women for sex, not for comfort. Yet he had fallen asleep next to her so easily.

Thirdly, there was no amount of alcohol he had consumed to blame it on. He had always needed a couple of glasses of whiskey to fuck, and even though he had told himself that the only reason he wanted to fuck Nadia so badly was because he broke his cardinal rule of mixing alcohol, now that he had, he was left with nothing but the truth.

He liked her, wanted her, and was starting to crave her after only knowing her for two days. Hell, the smell of her was becoming intoxicating, and that told him all he needed to know, because if he could care for her this much after two silly little days, what could he feel for the beautiful woman next to him after a week? A month? A year?

Suddenly, he got up, desperately in need of space. He was quiet as he threw on some clothes, unable to so much as look at her again, afraid if he did, he might crawl back in bed with her. It wasn't the regret that made him capable of leaving her; it was the grief and sorrow that had been eating away at him for years since his wife's passing.

He was going down the steps to find a place to sleep, either on one of the couches or a sun lounger out on the deck. Hell, he didn't care as long as he was alone—

"Dad?"

Dante stopped in his tracks to see his son coming in from the deck. "Why are you up?"

"Can't sleep," Leo told him, closing the sliding glass door. "You?"

"Can't sleep, either," Dante agreed.

"Right." Leo's face turned slightly suspicious. "Where are you going?"

He wanted to tell his son to stop asking questions and get his ass back to bed, but he knew that would only make him more suspicious. "To see the view at night. Same thing I'm sure you were doing, right?"

"Yes, but ... don't you have a better view than all of us on the balcony?" He pointed up the steps to Dante's quarters.

Dante flexed his jaw. It was much easier to lie to your kids when they were young. Now, all his kids were too damn smart for their own good.

Thinking quickly, he did the best he could. "Well, I wanted to go for a walk on the deck and see the view."

It seemed to have worked because he had Leo asking, "Want me to join yo—"

"No," Dante answered, probably a bit too quickly. "You go get some sleep."

"All right." Leo shrugged, passing him.

It had made Dante instantly feel worse than he was already feeling, but he knew if Leo had come with him, then at the end of their walk, he would have had no choice but to go back up to his room with Nadia. And that was something he didn't think he had the strength to do.

It was already going to be hard to resist her for the remainder of the weekend, with nothing but the smell of sunshine surrounding him. He couldn't promise he wouldn't sleep with her again, knowing he would use the excuse that it would be the last time. The fact that he was already envisioning them fucking again before she slipped back down to her room, along with the excuse he needed to do so, told him that it wouldn't be the last time. Nadia was the kind of woman whom you couldn't only fuck once. You needed seconds, and thirds ... each time tethering yourself to her until there was no escape.

No, his first with Nadia had to be his last.

He knew this, because he had experienced this feeling only one other time in his life. And he planned on keeping *his promise to love only one woman for the remainder of his. So, he would have to ignore Nadia from here on out, no matter how much it hurt to do it.*

"Oh yeah, Dad?" Leo called out to him before disappearing down the steps.

Dante turned to look at his son, who reminded him the most of his dead wife.

"Amo heard a scream, so I went to go check on Nadia in her room."

Swallowing hard, he knew exactly where this was going.

"But she wasn't in her room." Leo's lips lifted in a smile. "Don't worry; I covered for you, but you might want to tell Nadia that she screamed because she saw a spider."

He stared back at his son, confused, but then nodded.

"You're not going to go back up there, are you?" Leo asked knowingly, his smile disappearing.

Dante slowly shook his head this time, deciding to tell the truth.

Watching his son give him his back and walk away, he could feel the disappointment in Leo without a single word.

Dante didn't know what bothered him more—the fact he had just disappointed his own son yet again, or the fact his son was disappointed he wasn't going to give Nadia a chance.

Dante stared down at the shirt. The memory that had played in his mind hadn't been the one he had wanted to remember.

Tossing the items back down, he no longer gave as much care as Nadia had when she had handled them.

But sometimes, you are reminded with what you must never forget.

A BETTER CHANCE WITH POSEIDON

A strange smell entered Nadia's dream. She woke up groggy, scrunching up her nose, to find the smell wasn't in her dream at all. She sat up, and an ominous feeling overcame her, her instincts telling her something wasn't right.

Quickly, she got out of bed, grabbed her robe, and wrapped it around her tightly before opening her door. The strange smell only became stronger as she did so. It smelled like ...

Fuel?

She was now certain something was definitely wrong.

Adrenaline soaring through her, she hurriedly knocked on Leo's then Amo's doors, yelling, "Wake up!" loudly after she had tried to open their doors but found them locked.

She banged on the doors like their lives depended on it, her fist about to meet Amo's door once more, only for it to miss when it was suddenly swung open.

"Jesus Christ!" A sleepy Amo finally appeared. "Is there a spider in your room or somet—"

"No! What?" Nadia was confused by the spider

comment, but she didn't have time to wonder where the fuck that had come from. "Something's wrong. You smell that?" Her grave voice let him know the severity of her fears.

Amo simply sniffed the air once, and it was like the beast inside of him had awoken. Without a word, he went to Leo's door.

"It's locke—"

Using his arm to take the blow, he used his brute force to force it open before Nadia could even finish her word.

The sight of Amo frightened her. She had always seen him as a boy up until this moment, but now Nadia could see the soldier. It was like a beast had been locked away inside of him, waiting for its moment to break free.

Leo stood, shocked at the break-in. It was clear he had been throwing a shirt on, something that Amo hadn't had the luxury of doing. But once he took in their appearances, Leo immediately understood the severity of the situation as well.

"Let me get my shoes."

"No time," Amo said, grabbing his arm and jerking him forward. None of them were going to be wearing shoes for whatever they were about to face.

Passing Nadia, Amo did the same—grabbing her arm firmly and giving a silent order that they were to stick together.

Quickly, they took the steps up, and once they were on the floor of the indoor living room, they heard a noise coming from outside on the deck, causing them to freeze in place. It was like the sound of a garage opening.

"What is that?" Nadia whispered with a hard swallow.

"I don't know," Amo answered with a worrying tone in his voice. For a second, it was like you could see the brave beast slip to reveal that he, too, was becoming afraid for them.

The soldier's mind worked a mile per second, figuring out his next move, and then he suddenly decided. He brought Nadia's and Leo's hands together. "Wait here while I get Dante. I'll be back with him in a second. If something happens, you two run for it, right off this boat and into the ocean."

Nadia firmly nodded, as did Leo, all of them internally knowing they might have more of a fighting chance in the water than on the yacht. What was once a bright oasis to them all weekend was now beginning to feel more and more like a death trap. The eerie night making it feel like this might just be their burial site.

Certain they would listen to his order, Amo ran up the steps, and Nadia watched him until he disappeared.

It felt strange for her to take orders from Amo. She was much older; she should be the one to give orders and think about what they should do next, but something in her told her to trust the Caruso soldier. It came easy and felt safe to do so.

Nadia gave the hand in hers a squeeze that seemed more for herself than for him. Glancing over at the teenager, she thought it had been alarming to see Amo the way he was in dire situations, but seeing Leo was something different altogether ... more frightening. There was no concern or worry on his beautiful, young face. It was like she had seen *acceptance* for whatever was to come. Her depths going to the gauze covering where his eye should be, she could see how desperately it needed to be changed. It was stained with discharge and was starting to lift from where he must have slept on it after wearing it all day.

It was clear Leo no longer feared death. His accident

had rendered him dead inside already; therefore, there was nothing to fear. It seemed almost a blessing in this moment as Nadia's knees began to shake, but she knew better than to know it was actually a curse. It made her soul hurt even more for him, even though they might only have moments left to live, but she wished he knew how precious those moments could be.

Leo squeezed her hand in return, and, unlike Nadia, he kept his grip tight, not letting it falter.

It was like her shaky legs had suddenly stopped as they found the strength to stand firm. The boy gave her strength, sharing it between them selflessly, and that was when Nadia found peace, her gut telling her everything would be fine at the exact moment she heard running coming back down the steps from a returning Amo and Dante joining them.

The three men all gave a single look at each other, and Nadia found the comfort to know she was going to live then. The overwhelming certainty that they were going to make it out alive was a strange and profound feeling, but her gut just told her it would be so. And it was all because of the determined three before her. Whatever they were about to be faced with was going to be no match for them.

Dante and Amo led the charge, while Leo still held her hand tightly as they followed their backs to go see what the noise had been. They could hear muffled voices coming from below deck, and when they reached the railing quietly, they looked down into the ocean to see a tender was being deployed from its stowage.

"Hurry this thing up!" a voice hissed.

"I'm going as fast I can!" another one hissed.

"Well, I'd like to be fucking out of here when this thing blows!"

If it was even possible, Nadia's heart pounded harder.

Dante and Amo gave each other another knowing look as Amo pointed to his chest then to the tender below. Dante nodded in return, pointing to his chest then to Leo and Nadia. When they nodded, it wasn't a split-second later when their silent plan went into action, starting with Amo.

In one fast motion, Amo went over the railing, taking a dive into the ocean below and right beside the almost fully deployed tender.

"Now us," Dante announced once their cover was officially blown. They had clearly wanted Amo to have the element of surprise by making him go first.

"What? Jump?" Nadia looked at him like he was fucking crazy. "Like when I did before I almost drowned?"

"Exactly," Dante instructed. The voices of the ones already escaping told them that they had no time to do or get anything else. It was now or never.

Leo was already climbing to the other side of the railing.

A frustrated Dante pushed her to hurry. "You already did it wh—"

"Well, that was before I realized I couldn't swim—AH!" Suddenly, Nadia was lifted into his arms then tossed overboard. All she had heard was, "You lived," before she was surrounded by water.

Just as she was rising out of the water, two splashes erupted right beside her. It took her a second to catch her breath, coughing and blinking her eyes while she struggled to float.

It had been much different the first time she had jumped into the water. For one, it had been her choice to do so. Secondly, it was so dark now, and the ocean was a scary thing to be in at night.

Taking another wave straight to her face, she went

under, thinking this was going to be it for her, when arms surrounded her, pulling her up to the surface once more.

"You're fine," a soothing voice told her, beginning to pull her through the water. "Just relax."

Seeing it was Dante, she immediately did as she was told, knowing he had saved her from drowning before, so she trusted him enough to know this wasn't going to be any different.

Dante swam them toward the tender while Nadia focused on trying to keep her head above the water. She couldn't imagine the sheer strength he must've had for him to be able to do this, because Nadia was already exhausted just from trying to keep herself from taking on any more water.

They finally reached the tender, and she was grateful when Leo, who had already climbed on board, held out his hand for her to take. Nadia took it like it was the lifeboat and was shocked he managed to pull her out of the water soaking wet. She was not petite by any means, so she knew why Dante had to be the one to swim her to safety, as Leo was still quite young and hadn't filled out yet.

Being brought onboard the small boat, she helped Leo bring up his father, as he was much heavier.

"We gotta get the fuck out of here," Amo warned once they were all on. "Now!"

Nadia wiped the water from her eyes, coughing. She could see Amo's back while he appeared to be facing the culprits with their bloody hands covering their faces. The soldier had obviously been busy.

Dante sprang into action, moving to the wheel to drive them away from the yacht. Even though this tender looked like a really nice speedboat to her, it was like going from Buckingham Palace to a shack with all six people onboard.

When Leo went to help Amo hold them in place, Nadia was able to finally see who was responsible.

Max ... Lila?

She found herself more shocked by the latter, not believing the sweet woman could have done anything to hurt them. Well, whatever they had or hadn't done, she was about to find out as Dante cut the engine. He had brought them quite a distance away from the yacht once he was certain enough they were out of harm's way.

"Talk."

Nadia went from fearing for her life to Max's and Lila's by not only the anger in Dante's voice, but his frost-bitten gaze, and they were the ones who were wearing life jackets.

When the two sat there frozen, Amo picked Max up without warning, spun him around, and forced his upper half over the side, holding his head under the water. He pulled him back up for air with the vice grip he had on his hair.

"Now are you willing to talk?" Dante asked over his choking.

"Don't tell them, honey," Lila said with a muffled voice, still holding her nose. "They won't kill—"

Amo sunk Max's head back under once more, this time holding him there longer than he did last time.

Max came out of the water choking harder as the blood continued to spill from his own broken nose.

"Okay!" Max choked out, agreeing to talk in fear of being drowned.

Lila went to detest, but Max screamed at her, "Easy for you to say; you're not the one being fucking drowned!"

"I can give you a turn?"

Lila's mouth snapped close at Amo's warning.

"Now ..." Dante told him to get talking.

"The day you boarded, I was sent a text, along with fifty thousand dollars deposited into my bank account to kill everyone on the ship. They told me, after I did it, I would be deposited another fifty."

"A hundred thousand?"

She watched Dante utter the number in disappointment. It was quite obvious he thought his life alone was worth more than that, and Nadia was pretty sure he would have doubled the money for him *not to do it*.

Amo was just as hurt, throwing Max in for another dip.

"It was a hundred," Max came up out of the water, clarifying in deep breaths, "but I told them I would only do it if my girlfriend, Lila, could come with me and got her own hundred thousand dollars."

"How sweet ..." Nadia grumbled sarcastically.

Dante shared her sentiment but continued on, "Who sent the money?"

A nervous Max started stuttering, looking at Lila as she silently pleaded for him not tell. "I-I-If I tell you, I'm dead anyway."

"Okay, then." Amo started jerking off his lifejacket, and when he didn't reveal the name in the time it took for him to do so, he threw him off the boat. "Get to swimming."

"He didn't hurt anyone yet!" Nadia screamed at the soldier over Max's attempts of swimming away. She couldn't believe she ever thought Amo wasn't capable of hurting a fly. "Nothing's even been done to the ship ye—"

BOOM!

Staring at the flames in the distance, she quietly sat back down, knowing the chef and skipper were still onboard. Nadia didn't agree with it, but after that, she knew Max had a better chance with Poseidon than up here with the fucking mafia members whom he had almost just killed.

When Amo grabbed a crying Lila by her lifejacket, her mouth started moving a mile per minute.

"One-Shot! All they would tell us is they went by One-Shot! We were to cut the fuel line while everyone was sleeping, and that was it. We tried doing it the first night, but Nadia and Leo woke up and were talking. So, the next day, Max planned to get you all drunk, even told you their rum runners were virgin, but they weren't."

Suddenly, Nadia felt sick, sicker than anything she had witnessed tonight. The fact that they knew they were going to kill kids—well, at least she still viewed Leo as a kid—told her what kind of cruel people they were.

"That, of course, backfired when Nadia slept upstairs that night, because we weren't sure when you two would actually stop fucking and go to sleep."

Nadia's mouth hit the fucking deck, and what was worse was seeing Amo's eyes practically popping out of his sockets, while Leo didn't even react, meaning he had clearly already known.

"There was no spider, was there?" Amo asked, turning to Leo when something clicked together in his head.

Leo shook his head. "No."

Oh God, she cried inside her head, wishing she were swimming with the fishes alongside Max right about now, finally understanding the spider comment. *I should have stayed on the fucking boat.*

Covering her face with her hands, she looked at Dante through her fingers to see he hadn't been bothered by the revelation in the slightest.

"Okay." Amo cleared his throat, throwing a forever embarrassed Nadia a lifeline by continuing. "Go on."

"Tonight was our last chance, so when you all stayed in

your rooms and were separated, we ... well ... went for it," Lila finally finished.

"Anything else, boss?" Amo asked, looking at Dante.

"Nope."

With that, Amo flung the woman overboard.

"No!" Nadia shot up from where she sat. "She told you everything!"

"That's why I left her lifejacket on." Amo shrugged coldly. "She'll live ... if someone other than us comes to rescue her ass."

Going to protest, she suddenly heard something in the distance. "Shh!" Nadia urged.

Everyone stopped moving to carefully listen.

"That's just Lil—"

She shook her head. The noise was over Lila's swimming and much farther in the distance.

A quiet, "Help! Aide-moi!"

Before she could even get the words out, Amo was already getting behind the wheel.

Dante pulled her to sit down beside him, holding her close as the boat took off toward the yacht. With the flames illuminating everything around it, they were able to see a body holding on to the top of floating debris, and then they saw another person beside him the closer they got. The chef and skipper were alive.

She hadn't noticed how cold she was until that moment Dante wrapped an arm around her shoulders.

"Are you okay?" he asked, looking her over.

Nadia found herself shocked he was no longer ignoring her. "Yes, I'm fine."

"Sorry I threw you over," he said apologetically.

Nadia managed to chuckle, despite what had just happened. She figured she should still be mad, but it appeared, like him, she had clearly found a new perspective after what they had just gone through. "I'm sorry about your yacht."

"Oh yeah." Dante's gaze went to the fire getting closer, which happened to be burning up millions of dollars' worth. "It's not mine."

Her own eyes shot to his in surprise. "It's not?"

"Nope," he said, unbothered. "It belonged to Desmond Beck."

THE MOST DANGEROUS MAN IN KANSAS CITY

O nce Nadia had made it safely back to Kansas City, it was strange to be home from the moment she got off the plane. The plane ride had been nerve-racking, but she had found herself much calmer this time. On the way to Florida, it had not only been her first time flying, but she had been amongst strangers. This time, however, she felt amongst friends and was comforted in that fact.

But when it was time to land and the airplane door opened, she couldn't help but feel the bond they had formed over the weekend was beginning to slip. It was like making a type of friend over summer vacation that you normally wouldn't have gotten the chance to make, and when they went back to school, there was an awkward moment of goodbyes before you felt the sudden loss, both of you knowing you might not see each other until next year … if ever.

However, when the car went toward the casino hotel instead of taking her home, it appeared she was wrong about having to say goodbye just yet.

"Uh ... My apartment is that way." She pointed in the opposite direction.

Dante's face stayed impassive. "I'm aware."

"So ... I'd like to go home," she finished, as if it was silly that she even had to say them in the first place. Of course, she wanted to go home. She wanted a shower and to be in her own freaking clothes for once. Dante had purchased them each an outfit to come home in, as all their belongings were either in the ocean or burned to a crisp. Yes, the basic yet expensive jeans and T-shirt were nicer than anything she owned in her closet, but she still just wanted her own stuff back.

"There's been an issue. We need to go to my casino first."

Silence filled the car for the rest of the ride.

Nadia didn't know what to think, but she got this instinctual feeling that whatever "issue" it was, it must've involved her; otherwise, why would he be bringing her along?

A little tingling of fear grew in her at not knowing what had possibly happened to make this never-ending roller coaster of a ride worse. Nadia just really wished she had her phone to check on Haley. She was sure she was worried by now.

The many possible scenarios filled her head as they got to Dante's casino hotel and took the trek she had made just Friday, which now seemed like a lifetime ago.

Walking through the casino, going up the elevator, and heading to his office felt much different this time around. The first time, she had been slightly nervous, afraid that she wouldn't walk out with the donation she needed. This time, however, she was smart enough to be afraid for her life.

When Dante opened his office door and held it open for

her to enter first, she walked through slowly, frightened of the man who sat behind the huge wooden desk. She remembered walking in and seeing Dante in that same spot, but not even Dante's icy exterior compared to this one's foreboding one. The chill that went up her spine traveled all the way from her fingertips down to her toes. Her gift of intuition screamed for her to run, while his strange, blue-green gaze beckoned her to come closer, telling her that, if she took even one step in the opposite direction, it just might be her last, and that was when she knew exactly who she was face-to-face with ... *The Boogieman.*

The second she knew she needed out of here was the same second Amo and Leo walked in as well, closing the door behind them. There was certainly no escaping now, as she had to keep herself from shivering in his presence. The wickedness in him affected her more than a usual person, and that was saying a lot, because she was certain there wasn't anyone who wanted to look him in the eyes.

The smile that tugged up one side of his lips made him appear even more handsome than he already was, but for her, it served only as a reminder of just how dangerous he was.

"Ms. Brooks, it's nice to meet you." He waved a hand for her to sit down.

She could feel his strange gaze taking her in as she sat. Being looked at by men was nothing new to a woman, but he didn't look at her like men usually did. He looked at her curiously, like she was under a microscope and he was simply trying to find out everything and anything about her in a single glance.

Frankly, she didn't know which way would be worse for The Boogieman to look at her.

"Scoot," Dante told him, motioning for him to get out of

his chair, making Nadia look at the perplexing pair. The second she saw the two side-by-side, she knew before he spoke his next words. "Nadia, this is my oldest son … Lucca."

She found herself frozen like a statue, not believing she hadn't seen the resemblance at first. It was certainly blatantly obvious now. Knowing he was one of his sons, she was only shocked by the fact that it was Lucca. From what they had said about him, she would have never guessed he was the one all of Kansas City was frightened of.

"Nice to meet you," she managed to get out.

"Scoot," Dante told him again when his son continued to stare at her. "And are you going to tell me what it is that couldn't wait till the fucking morning?"

"Yes." He continued to stare at her a moment longer then stood to let his father take his place.

She was grateful to finally be released from his gaze, but it was short-lived when he threw a newspaper down on the desk.

Being closer, Dante didn't need to pick up the paper to see what was plastered on the front page of *The Kansas City Tribune*.

Is that …?

"Oh, my fucking God!" Nadia screamed, picking up the paper off the desk to see herself in black and white. But it wasn't just an innocent picture of her; it was a picture of her in a bathtub while Dante stared down at her. Someone on that passing cruise ship had taken a picture of them at the perfect moment, making them appear more than they were … Well, more than a one-time thing.

"Holy shit." Amo came closer to get a look. "I gotta see thi—"

Nadia quickly folded the paper out of his view and smacked him with it.

Leo continued to stand quietly, but with a smile now, while Lucca began to curiously stare at her again.

When Amo jumped back, she opened the paper again to take another look at her humiliation, managing now to look past the photo to see the headline.

HAS THE CASINO KING CHOSEN HIS QUEEN?

"Oh my God ..." she cried again, the pit in her stomach about to make her sick.

"When was this?" Dante slid the paper out of her hands, keeping her from staring at it a moment longer, to see the date.

"Today's paper," Lucca informed him. "And I'm sure you'll get the front page again tomorrow due to the boat blowing up."

"Get the editor in chief on the phone and remind him who he really fucking works for," Dante ordered fiercely.

His son nodded.

Dante now looked at Amo. "I want you and Drago to switch off guarding Nadia until we find One-Shot."

Amo went to firmly nod his own head when Lucca spoke up.

"Drago's not going back to bodyguarding anytime soon. He has his wife to worry abou—"

"That was an order," Dante boomed as he hit the desk with his fist.

Nadia could see it then, as the ice-blue eyes battled

against the blue-green ones. The shift of power that was trying to be out won from father to son. It didn't take a rocket scientist to know that Lucca must've been his underboss, and he sought the chair his father sat in. She just wondered how much longer it was going to be before the bloodshed. And for bloodshed to happen against your own family, of those you once loved, was a crime of the highest accord. It was simply unforgivable.

Nadia would know because she had survived it.

The boss' tone shifted, his order now coming out as a plea. "Please, just ask Drago. I'm sure you could figure something out to keep Katarina protected while he's with Nadia."

"I don't think One-Shot will go for Kat again. I think, after that," Leo finally spoke up, pointing at the paper that sat on his father's desk, "Nadia might be next, especially if she's an easy target with no guard. She needs the best," he warned his brother gravely.

Whoever Drago was, she could only imagine he was the best of the Caruso men, right along with Amo, who had proven himself on the yacht.

Lucca seemed taken aback by Leo's response, moving his eyes to his younger brother's. It was like they spoke to each other without words before he nodded, agreeing to do it.

"Thank you," Dante said with relief.

If it was possible, blue-green eyes went back to staring at her even more curiously, making her head spin more than it already was with how they were talking about her as if she wasn't in the room.

"Dante, can I talk with you?" Nadia interjected quietly. "Alone."

None of the men waited to hear Dante's response, beginning to leave.

"See you soon," Amo told her.

Leo, however, paused at the door, turning to give her a last good look. "Bye, Nadia."

"Bye, Leo." She waved at him with sadness in her heart. She couldn't help but feel hurt to see him leave when she just wanted more time to help him.

Waiting until he was completely gone from view, she finally turned back around to face Dante, only to see Lucca still standing there, closely watching her. He did so a moment longer before he spoke.

"It was nice meeting you, Ms. Brooks." His eyes glowed as a slow smile curved his lips. "I hope to see you around."

Those words should have scared her, coming from The Boogieman. However, there was no chill that went up her spine when he had said them, seeing he had genuinely meant them. Whatever had just taken place, she wasn't quite sure what to think, other than she strangely got the approval of the most dangerous man in Kansas City.

"Nice meeting you, too, Lucca."

She watched him quietly disappear and couldn't help but think what it would have been like to *not* have gotten his approval.

Dante got right to it, without hearing what she had wanted to talk to him about. "You can stay here at the hotel. I have a roo—"

"No," Nadia said, stopping him.

"No?" He looked at her, not comprehending what she must be referring to. "No, what?"

"As in, no, I'm not staying here. I haven't been home in days," she clarified. "I just want to go home and sleep in *my* bed and in *my* clothes."

Stunned, Dante clearly hadn't considered what she might want. It took him a few seconds to get his thoughts in order. "Okay, Amo will take you home, then, and stay with you for tonight."

Nadia shook her head. "Your men are clearly spread thin. He can take me home, but I'll be okay for tonight. Haley is my roommate, so it's not like I'll be alone. Besides" —she looked at the godforsaken newspaper—"whoever it is wanting to kill you won't know we're back till tomorrow."

Opening his mouth, he then quickly closed it before he seemed to say something else entirely as he went around the desk to stand in front of her. "If this is about the paper, fuck the paper."

"Dante, I run Moonbeam; how am I supposed to get donors after—"

"Donors are not going to be a problem," he assured her.

Angry with his nonchalant response, Nadia went for the door.

"I'm sorry." Dante grabbed her arm, stopping her from taking another step. "I'm sorry I dragged you into *any* of this," he apologized sincerely, bringing her closer to him and resting his head on hers.

Nadia's breath hitched. It was the closest they had been since …

She took a deep breath, trying not to go back to that night on the yacht. She needed to keep her head straight enough to leave.

"Listen, this is a lot. I just need to go home and clear my head, okay? I can come back tomorrow, and we can talk about *this* after a good night's rest." She emphasized the word *this* for whatever the hell was happening between them. They had yet to talk about what they were or if there was even a possibility of them. But she was sure Dante didn't even know himself yet.

Slowly, he nodded his head against hers then pulled away to let her leave. "Good night, Nadia."

She thought watching Leo tell her goodbye was hard, but this was excruciating, and they weren't even saying bye; it was just for one night. "Good night, Dante."

WAIVING AMO GOODBYE, SHE UNLOCKED HER apartment door, only to be tackled as soon as the door was closed.

"I've been worried sick." A familiar, sweet woman squeezed her to death for an eternity before she pulled away and started hitting her. "You scared the shit out of me, Nadia!"

"I'm sorry." She laughed, trying to dodge the love hits. "I sent you a text saying I lost my phone, but I was all right!"

"You're supposed to be the responsible one. How could you lose your phone?"

"Yeah, well, it's surprisingly not hard when you're getting shot at." The smart comeback slipped through her lips.

"What?" Haley suddenly stopped hitting her. "You were shot at?"

"Yes—"

Nadia got the breath knocked out of her when Haley grabbed her for a hug again. "But I'm fine," she assured her best friend that she didn't even get a scratch on her.

"Thank God!" Haley cried then pulled herself together. "What the hell happened?"

Nadia was able to answer simply, "Dante Caruso happened."

Her friend's mouth dropped open. Then, seeming to remember something, she went to the coffee table and picked up today's paper. "Oh, I know."

Going over, she slipped the paper from Haley's hand and took a seat on the couch, staring down at it ominously. "Yeah, well, he gives Tony Montana a run for his money."

"Spill," Haley said, sitting down next to her.

Knowing Haley would go to her grave with what she would tell her, she spilled everything that had happened since she had walked into the hotel casino on Friday to today, letting her know that the rumors about Dante Caruso were true.

There were several moments of silence after she got done with her story while Haley took in everything she had said before she spoke. "Do you know what you're going to do or say to him tomorrow?"

Nadia shook her head, staring down at the black and white photo again. "I think I really like him," she finally admitted, more to herself than to Haley. "But I don't think he'd ever care for me the way I feel myself beginning to care for him." It was true and blatantly obvious that the man she was falling for in a mere weekend had already given his heart away to another woman many years ago, his heart that was now buried along with her.

"You sure about that?" Haley asked softly, pointing at Dante's face in the photo.

As she let her eyes drift, her heart skipped a beat. She had been so focused on herself in the bathtub, as it was humiliating to be undressed on the front page of the newspaper in her city, that she hadn't really gotten a good look at him.

The way Dante looked at her was the way any woman would dream to be looked at. There was so much care, tenderness, and ... love in a single look that it had Nadia wanting to run back to the casino hotel right now.

"By the way, you forgot to mention how hot he was in that folder of yours that you made of him. I would have picked him if I kne—"

"Desmond!" Nadia gasped, remembering Haley had had her own meeting. "How did it go?"

"Well ..." Haley started, not knowing where to begin, "I think I might have gotten you more than just a donation."

"What?" Nadia screamed in excitement. "Spill!"

"I will, but not tonight," she told her. "Your story is enough for one night, so we'll save mine and Desmond's for another day. Now, I'm going to bed before you make me spoil it." Haley laughed, quickly starting to leave. She knew if she stayed there, Nadia would have it out of her in five minutes, and they needed to get some rest.

"No fair!" Nadia yelled at her friend before she disappeared behind her bedroom door. The silence hit her hard, reminding her that she was finally alone.

Nadia slowly brought her eyes back to the black and white photo. Only she no longer saw herself in it anymore.

Had he been looking at her like this the entire time, and she had simply missed his glances? Or did the photographer snap the picture at the perfect moment, making it look like more than it was?

I have one night to decide.

MARIA FUCKING CARUSO

Getting to sleep had been hard for Nadia, but she had woken up this morning refreshed and knew exactly what she had to do. She now walked onto the casino floor with a clear mind, planning to go through with her decision. After she hit the elevator button with certainty, it took several moments before it dinged, and the doors slid open. The person on the other side had her star bound ...

"Hello." The beautiful woman in five-inch heels smiled brightly. "It's Nadia, right?"

The little girl in Nadia, who had been bullied by beautiful girls in the past, wanted to wait for the next elevator, but grown Nadia had learned to handle herself, so she took a step onto the elevator. "Yes. And you are?" she asked, really hoping it wasn't one of Dante's women who had been sexting him.

"Sorry." She laughed, realizing how weird it might've come off that she knew her name before they were introduced. "I'm Maria. Maria Caruso."

Oh, thank God. Nadia breathed, suddenly feeling the

warmth come off the girl. "You must be ... Dante's daughter?"

"Yep." She smiled, raising a perfect brow. "Who did you think I was?"

"Honestly, I was scared you might've been one of Dante's—" She paused, not knowing the proper word for "one of his booty calls."

"Oh no." Maria practically gagged in understanding. "He's my dad, but not that kind of *dad*."

"Okay, good." Nadia laughed it off, knowing a girl Maria's age would consider a guy at Dante's age a daddy.

"Yep, you're totally safe with me," Maria assured her. Then, moving to the elevator buttons, she lit one up that would take them down instead of going to the top to Dante's office.

"Uh ... I was actually on my way to see your fath—"

"I actually thought we could hang out for a bit." The woman's teeth sparkled even brighter. "I've heard so much about you from Leo and Amo. I'd love to get to know you myself."

Nadia swallowed hard, looking at the numbers falling to the basement floor. She had never been so frightened of a woman until this fucking moment. It was weird to fear a tall, legged blonde goddess in a dress, but something in her told her to run, like it had with Lucca. Honestly, maybe more so, because if there was one thing women knew how to do, it was how to hurt another woman much worse than any man ever could.

Maria fucking Caruso looked like she belonged to the plastics on *Mean Girls* ... except somehow richer and prettier. No, worse than that. It looked like she ate Regina George for fucking breakfast.

"I-I-I should really go see him." Her survival instincts

tried to kick in to save her, but the gorgeous girl wasn't having it.

Maria locked her arm with Nadia's just in time for the elevator door to *ding* open. "Oh, he can wait. Plus, I have something fun to show you."

She really, really, really didn't want to walk down the dark hallway she was faced with, but Maria began dragging her toward a door that was waiting at the end. Listening to the girl's stilettos hit the floor, she walked down, arm-in-arm with her, not knowing what to fucking do.

Dante's offspring were not only turning out to be more good-looking than him but were quite honestly terrifying. She was sure she would rather take on The Boogieman again than this psychotic princess.

Sensing her nerves, Maria spoke but continued dragging her along. "I was so jealous I couldn't join you on the yacht last weekend ..."

"Uh-huh," Nadia said, glancing back at the elevator ... for it to already be gone. *How the fuck do I always end up in these situations?*

"But, you know, I'm married, and my husband and I haven't even been apart for a day since."

It was everything Nadia could do to stay polite and calm as Maria flashed her huge diamond ring.

"I-It's beautiful."

Christ, if Regina George was fucking real, she was with the thing that fucking spawned her.

"Thanks." She smiled so sweetly before banging on the door like she was a prison guard bringing in a prisoner.

To think that One-Shot was going to be the one to take her out was a joke. It was the fucking Victoria Secret model who was going to be the one to brutally murder her.

The door flung open, and a big, suited guy stood on the

other side, not looking happy to see Maria, but he moved to the side nonetheless for her to enter.

Nadia couldn't believe what she was looking at. It was another casino full of tables and risqué-dressed women all over. This casino, she was sure, was the best kept secret in all of Kansas City.

Still holding her arm, Maria said hi to the passing lingerie-clad women as if she was on a first name basis with them all. As she sat them at an empty blackjack table, Nadia could see she had no reason to fear for her life at all with the woman. She was the friendliest girl she had possibly ever met—

"You wish." Maria flashed her left hand and shiny rock, practically taking a man's eye out when he leaned too closely to her so he could whisper in her ear.

When his eyes drifted over to Nadia, then, her next words came out as a hiss, "Does she look familiar? Or did you happen to miss yesterday's paper."

Realization hit the man like a Mack truck.

The blonde's pouty lips lifted into a wicked smile. "Unluckily for you, you happen to not only hit on his girlfriend, but his daughter in one fell swoop."

Now the man looked like he was going to shit himself. "I-I'm sorry. Please tell your fath—I mean, Mr. Caruso—I apologize."

"Hmm ..." Maria tapped her chin with a manicured nude nail. "I'll think about it."

Correction: Maria eats men for breakfast.

Nadia would have a reason to fear for her life if she were a man, but luckily for her, she wasn't. This poor sucker, however, wasn't as lucky.

"That's your cue to leave," came from a female voice.

When the man scurried off, Nadia turned to see the

woman who now stood on the dealer side of the table. Snickering with Maria, she was a different kind of a man's dream of a woman than Maria was. Where the blonde bombshell was a tall, legged, sophisticated woman, fit for a runway, the dealer was every horndog's wet dream—short, curvy for days, and had a pair of tits on her that Hugh Hefner would have wanted plastered on the cover of the next issue of *Playboy*. It would undoubtedly be a bestseller, too, and Nadia herself would purchase it.

"I'm Sadie, the pit boss," she introduced herself with a fast shuffle of the deck. "But for Maria, I go back to dealing just for her."

Watching Sadie take several hundred-dollar chips out of the tray to place in front of the blonde, she didn't want to hold them up. "I'm sorry. I don't have anything on me. I lost my purse the other day, and I didn't think I'd be gambling when I came here."

"Oh no, you will not be paying to gamble in my father's casino," Maria said, halving her chips and placing them in front of Nadia. "He owes you a lot more than this for getting you plastered on the front page of *The Kansas City Tribune*."

"That's right." Sadie nodded firmly in agreement before giving her a wink. "Plus, what good is it to be the boss' new girlfriend if it doesn't come with perks?"

"Oh ... I'm not ..." Nadia couldn't even say the words, knowing a one-night stand with the man was far from being called his girlfriend.

"Honey, we *all* saw the picture." Sadie's tone matched a mother's telling her daughter that she knew everything there was about love. "If he's not asked you to be his girl, he will soon."

Maria simply bobbed her head in agreement, like the

best friend who was telling her that her mother was, in fact, right.

"Oh God." Nadia's head fell to the table, her mind that was once clear wavered back into a jumbled mess.

"Don't worry, honey. You came to the right place." The pit boss assured her before yelling to a passing waitress, "Cherry, two tequilas and two waters!"

Maria patted her back in comfort. "Yeah, Sadie's the woman whisperer. She'll sort you right out."

"That's right. I sorted Maria out, and now look at her. She's married to the second finest man in all of Kansas City." Confidence slipped through the pit boss' lips.

Again, Maria held up the big diamond as proof on her left hand.

"It's beautiful," Nadia told the girl again so she would finally put it down.

"Wait—who's the first?" Maria went back to Sadie, catching that she had called her husband only the *second* finest man in Kansas City.

"Oh, buttercup"—Sadie tapped the tip of Maria's perfect nose—"I love you and all, but if I told ya, then I'd have to kill ya. Now, how is Dom doing?"

"Good." Maria laughed, letting her drop it. "He's still perfect, of course."

Nadia said a silent prayer for the man named Dom. Within the ten minutes she had known Maria, she was a handful and probably had the schmuck by the ball—

"Oh, I know," Sadie said in agreement, clearly approving of her choice in husband. As she was dealing out the cards, it was starting to feel like an AA meeting for girls. "Unfortunately for all of us, we got it bad for a man."

Ugh, she was right. Nadia slammed her head back on the desk.

"Just in time," Sadie announced when two shots, along with the waters, appeared on the table. "Drink up. It'll give you some clarity."

"You can have mine, too," Maria told her, sliding her shot of tequila closer to Nadia.

Sadie's brow lifted in suspicion. "What? Are you pregnant?"

"No ..." The blonde quickly tapped the table to hit her thirteen. "I'm just not drinking tonight."

"Well, me neither." Nadia slid the shots back to the blonde. "Last time I drank ... I just have to keep my wits about me this time."

Now Sadie's suspicious gaze went to Nadia, seeming to know exactly what she meant.

Rolling her eyes, she picked up the two shots, downing one and then the other like it was simply water. Whatever love life problem Nadia was having, it looked like it paled to Sadie's in comparison. Maria's, however, was clearly as perfect as her and the twenty-one she had just made by receiving an eight of hearts.

Hitting her twelve didn't go quite as perfectly as Maria's had, busting with a face card. Then, when it was Sadie's turn to reveal her house card, she had a six hiding underneath, forcing her to hit and get another face card, making the house bust. The analogy was almost a perfect representation of their love lives.

Maria beamed as Sadie slid over her winnings.

"Perfect twenty-one and Dominic Luciano. Girl, you just can't lose."

Nadia had been taking a drink of her water and practically spit it all over the table. *Dominic Luciano?*

"You okay?" Maria asked her with concern.

"Mmhmm ..." she choked out. "You mean, Luciano as in ..." *The fucking rival mafia family in Kansas City?*

It was Sadie who answered in understanding. "That's the one."

Oh, this girl, Maria, had it out for every man, including her father. She was sure ... "I don't take it your father took that very well."

"No, he did not," Maria assured her, but Nadia didn't miss the hint of sadness in her voice. On the outside, it looked like Maria's life was perfect, but it was clear that even a girl who had everything still had some scars deep down.

"Want me to hurt him for you?" Nadia asked, knowing her father had hurt her in some way.

The beautiful blonde laughed at the joke, and the sadness that didn't belong on a girl like her left. "Thanks for the offer, but something tells me Karma might just be catching up to him." The way Maria was looking at her made Nadia feel like *she* was said *Karma*.

"You going to place your bet, hon?" Sadie reminded her to move a new chip in the circle.

"No, I think I'm done." She sighed, giving Maria back her chips.

The pit boss placed her hands on her hips. "What's wrong?"

"Honestly, I hate gambling," Nadia confessed to the girls. It had ruined so many of the kids' lives who went through her charity due to their parents' addiction. It made her feel so guilty to even be here.

"Oh, girl, I am so rooting for you." Sadie laughed along with an agreeing Maria.

Her not liking casinos, or gambling, for that matter,

seemed to be that bit of Karma that Maria was looking for, after all.

Sadie began dealing just for Maria. "So, what's the plan?"

"The plan?" Nadia asked her, confused.

"The plan of coming here today? Do you know what you're going to say to him?"

Damn, Sadie really was the woman whisperer. She knew exactly why she was fucking here and didn't even need to hear it. It must've been written all over her torn face.

Taking a deep breath, Nadia decided to fuck it and confide in them, but before she could, a cold familiar voice greeted them.

"Hello, ladies."

Seeing Lucca Caruso for the second time wasn't quite as jarring as the first. Nadia found herself no longer fearing The Boogieman; she could see past the man to the child beneath. Like in Leo, she could see the trauma, but it wasn't marred on the outside. It was deep and hidden beneath the wicked darkness, yet it was still there all the same, like it had been with Maria. Had their father been the cause of all their pain?

"I hate to interrupt, but Dante would like to see you now."

Yikes. Him being on a first-name basis with his father told her about all she needed to know.

"You ready?" His dark voice ominously asked her when she hadn't made a move.

Thankful that she hadn't taken that shot of tequila, she wondered if the three pairs of eyes staring at her could see the fear and nerves on her face.

Managing to finally muster up the courage, she finally

nodded and stood up from the chair. Was it weird that this felt like it was going to determine the rest of her life?

"Good luck, girl." Sadie winked at her.

Maria, however, stopped her from leaving and, for the first time, Nadia got a good look at her bright, emerald-green gaze that matched the green in her older brother's.

"I may be rooting for you just so you can turn his life upside down," Maria began confessing as harsh words spilled for her pretty lips, "but I can already tell he doesn't deserve you."

That revelation from his daughter sent Nadia's already fucked-up mind in a tailspin. So much so that she missed the odd look between Lucca and Maria before he started to walk her out, and the room full of people parting to give him a wide berth.

It wasn't until she was faced with Dante's door that everything stopped, and it was just ...

Clear.

I WILL HAUNT YOU

Walking into Dante's office, she hadn't expected it, but her heart had skipped a beat upon seeing him again. However, with the look of his icy exterior, she doubted his had done the same.

Seeing him start to get up, she stopped him. "You can stay there. This won't take long."

"This won't take long?" he questioned, stunned, and froze in place from rising out of his chair.

"Yes." She waited for him to slowly lower himself back down to his chair before she began. "I don't know what you planned to say to me, whether you were going to ask to see me again or not, but when I leave this office ... it will be the last time you see me."

It was easier this way, because if she heard him say he no longer wanted to see her, it would break her heart. But what would hurt even worse was if he did ask to see her again. Then she wouldn't have the strength to do this.

Nadia couldn't see anything in his hardened face, only the slight flex to his jaw.

"May I ask why?"

"I hate casinos."

"You hate casinos?" he asked, confused more than ever.

"Exactly." She nodded firmly.

"Then don't play in my casino. I don't care." Dante seemed to have an easy fix, but when Nadia shook her head, telling him it wasn't that easy, he continued, "I'm sorry, but I'm not understanding why that means you plan to never see me again once you hit that door?"

"We're two different people—" It was him this time who was going to interrupt her, but she wasn't done. Softly, she spoke the words containing the hard truth, "And you're in love with someone else."

Dante sat back in his chair, knowing exactly who she meant. "I will always love my wife. It's not like she walked out on me, Nadia. She died ... because of me."

"I know you will, and I wouldn't want that to ever change," Nadia said, taking a breath. "But you're not willing to share that love with anyone else, and as amazing as that night was with you, I know that's all you could ever give me, and it would never be enough."

She had to look past him now, the words too much for herself to bear saying, and Nadia couldn't witness the pain beginning on his face from talking about his wife. "You can blame yourself for her death all you want, Dante, but she knew the consequences of being with you ... just like I do, which is why ... I can't. I don't choose a life where I will wonder if my next step will be my last, or if you don't pick up the phone, it might mean you're dead." She spoke the name of the ghost that haunted his ice-blue eyes. "Melissa did ... I don't."

Dante stared at her for several moments, having to take in what she said, and when he finally went to open his mouth, there was a knock on the office door before it flung open.

One of his men, holding a folder, paused upon seeing her. "Oh, sorry, I—"

"That's okay. I was just leaving," Nadia said, wiping away the tear that had fallen before she turned for the door.

Standing from his chair, Dante waved his man on. "Sal, can you give us a minute?"

"No, please stay," Nadia urged him, and the man didn't know what to do, but she kept him in place when she went to the door herself. "Tell your men I can make it home myself, and that I won't be needing their services." Turning, she gave one last look at the man who had stolen her heart and would never be able to give his in return. "Goodbye, Mr. Caruso."

DANTE FELL BACK DOWN IN HIS CHAIR, WATCHING where she had just disappeared without giving him a single chance.

"Sir ..."

"Sal, give me a fucking minute!" Dante yelled at his soldier, who quietly left, closing him in alone with nothing but his thoughts and a memory he had hidden deeply ...

"Where is your mom?" Dante asked a young Maria as she came running in with her pink floppy dress from the direction of the kitchen.

Melissa had said she was going to take a nap while Leo was having his, so he had gone to his study to take care of a few business matters that were important, or he would have taken one with her.

Dante gave a silent curse at the missed opportunity. His wife and he hadn't been able to have one since Leo's birth.

Maria brushed her golden locks out of her face. "Have you checked her garden?"

"Tell Lucca to start dinner. I don't want your mother extending herself any more than she needs to." His son was only a young teenager, but his mother had already taught him well enough that he didn't need supervision to cook anymore.

Walking outside, the crisp air, along with the beautiful scents of her blooming flowers, caressed him. He always loved the smell back here. It was exactly how she smelled.

Glancing around, he was almost ready to go back inside when he caught sight of his wife on a ladder at the side of the gazebo, fiddling with a hanging planter well above on her head. Dante started running when her fingers brushed against the heavy glass planter and it wobbled.

As he snatched Melissa off the ladder, the planter fell down, crashing to the ground.

"What in the hell are you doing?"

"Shh ... One of the children will hear you."

"Don't shush me. They've heard much worse from me."

"Which you have promised to work on," she reminded him.

"Why are you on the ladder? You could have asked me or Lucca."

"I didn't want to disturb you." Peeling herself away from him, she went to get a broom and a dustpan from the gardening shed.

Fuming, he had to wait until she came back before laying into her again. Taking the broom and pan away from her, he started sweeping up the shattered glass.

"You don't think me finding my wife with her head bashed in would disturb me?"

"You're overreacting. It was a simple mishap. Don't make more of it than it was."

His overwhelmingly beautiful wife gave him a censuring glance.

"I'm not overreacting. What would I do without you?" It bothered him to his core to even think about that possibility.

"I have every confidence you would raise our four children with all the love you are capable of."

His brows furrowed at her choice of words. "What does that mean?"

"You're not a very demonstrative man, Dante. We've discussed this many times before."

Dropping the shards of glass in a waste bin, he leaned the broom against the gazebo before taking his wife into his arms.

"I love you."

"You do now, but you didn't when we married." She wrapped her arms around him. "We weren't given the choice to choose."

"Would you have chosen me?"

"Yes, once I got to know you better. Would you have chosen me?"

"If I didn't want you, I would have told my father to choose another bride for me," he hedged. "I loved you within the first month of our marriage. Just because I wasn't the one who picked you doesn't mean my love is less than a man's who was able to choose."

"Dante, from the moment you told me you loved me, I've never doubted your love for me, or our children. The problem we have is your inability to express your love to others the way you do to me."

"Our children know I love them."

"Do they? I worry about Lucca."

"You should be more concerned about yourself. If I ever see you climbing a ladder again ..."

"Why? You would never lay a hand on me regardless of how angry you are with me." Patting his cheek, Melissa moved out of his arms. "Leo will be waking. I need to go check on him. Come with me?"

Dante took her hand to creep inside the nursery next to their bedroom. Lovingly smiling at the small infant gurgling in his crib, Melissa picked the baby up to carry Leo to a rocking chair.

Going to their bedroom, he filled a glass with ice and opened a bottle of sparkling water, filling it up. Carrying it into the nursey, he gave it to Melissa as she nursed Leo.

"You take such good care of me. You've been a good husband."

"What brought that on?"

"I started thinking. You were right; I shouldn't have climbed the ladder. The basket was too high. Most accidental deaths happen in the home, by people just doing things that would have been wiser for them not to do. I'm sorry. I didn't mean to frighten you."

"Thank you. That still doesn't get you off the hook."

"I didn't expect it to." Melissa gave him one of her gentle smiles, which never failed to make him feel as if he was the luckiest son of a bitch on Earth that she had grown to love him. "I have to admit; I'm always so worried about your safety, I didn't take into account your feelings if something were to happen to me."

"I would be completely lost without you," he said with a hitch in his breath. Even saying it took away his ability to breathe.

"You're overreacting again. You could never be lost. You would be unhappy for a while, then I think you would find *another woman to love. You have my permission to remarry if you do."*

"The same permission won't be coming from me if I die."

"I would never remarry. No one would be able to compare to you."

He couldn't disagree with that, so he didn't try.

"I won't, either." His hand went to his heart as he made the pledge. "My eyes will never show love for another woman, my lips will never kiss another's, and my voice will never tell another woman of my love for her. I will only give those promises to you."

Her loving eyes grew sad. "Dante, if it does happen, and you do fall in love, please remember what I said. I would never want you to be alone. One day, the children will leave the home we made for them, and autumn leaves will continue to fall as we grow older. I couldn't be happy in Heaven if you were alone without someone to love."

"Let's change the subject. We're going to have to agree to disagree."

"Just promise me one thing, and we can talk about something else."

Dante knew Melissa wouldn't stop until she got out what she wanted to say.

"What do you want me to maybe promise you?"

"I want you to promise me … when you do want to remarry, that you love her before you put a ring on her finger."

Dante glared at Melissa when she said want. He was done with the conversation.

"I will," he said without meaning it.

"Dante Caruso, say I promise."

"No."

"I will haunt you if you don't."

He laughed. "Go ahead. I'm not afraid of ghosts."

"Please ... Dante. I promise never to climb a ladder again."

"I promise, only because I know you're going to outlive me ..."

He was forced to eat his words eight years later. His beautiful Melissa in a coffin because of him had marked his soul and heart forever. Autumn leaves had fallen without her by his side, and he swore he would remain alone until his dying day. He wasn't concerned about the promise he had given Melissa; he wasn't capable of loving another woman, so the promise had been null and void, just like his life was. So, he had let himself forget that sad memory and had let his life pass him by in a blur, with their children growing older and making lives for themselves.

In the quietness of the air, Dante thought he heard the sound of someone weeping. Thinking he was imagining things, he pushed it out of his mind until he gradually heard the weeping fade away.

Droplets hit the windowpane behind him, having him swivel in his chair. The beautiful, sunny day had turned cloudy, and the sky was beginning to rain. It was like watching teardrops quietly slide down the window until it pounded and beat at the glass. Melissa had once told him that God showed His anger with thunder, but it was the angels you had to tread softly around, for their tears could actually touch you.

"Darling, you can be mad all you want," he said out loud to the empty room. "I'm not afraid of ghosts."

No, it was a black-haired woman who terrified him.

"Nadia ... Nadia!"

Nadia had been walking at a practical jog, trying to get the hell out of there in case Dante or one of his men came after her. And even though she had come to care for the boy who was yelling after her, she wasn't sure she was strong enough to keep a brave enough face. However, having to wait for the elevator gave her no choice.

"We found your purse," Leo said, slightly out of breath from having to run to catch up with her.

"Oh ..." Nadia took the outstretched purse. "Thanks."

Leo's brows drew together, not missing the hurt she was desperately trying to hide. "You're not planning to see my farther again ... are you?"

She could only slowly shake her head, afraid her voice would betray her and the crying that she just barely held at bay would start.

When the elevator door dinged open, she walked through, raising her hand to wave the boy goodbye ... for the last time.

Dante stared down at the folder Sal had given him.

Sal was known to the world as The Great Salvatore, and to the government as the biggest pain in their asses. He might've been a world-renowned hacker, but to Dante, he was Salvatore Lastra, the boy he had picked up off the street many moons ago. It was the exact person whom Nadia had spoken of that had Dante opening his wallet to give her the donation to Moonbeam.

He had been good to the kid, arguably better and more of a father to Sal than he had been to his own kids, but that was because looking at Sal never reminded him of *her*. In return of the good fortune Dante had given him, Sal had joined the Caruso family and did things for him none of his other men could possibly dream of doing behind a computer screen. The folder he stared down at that contained probably everything he ever needed to know about Nadia Brooks was one of them.

Opening it, he noticed the first thing that was written about Nadia was that she was of Greek descent. That explained a lot of the similarities yet differences between them, like why her tanned skin was more bronze and why her athletic body looked like it had been chiseled. However, that was as far as he had gotten when his door barged open for the second time.

"What the fuck did you do?"

Dante looked up from his desk to see his youngest son. "What *I* did?" he asked harshly, knowing he must've passed Nadia on her way out. "She didn't give me the chance to say or do anything!"

"Well, I certainly didn't see you chasing after her!"

Even though his son's response might've been harsh itself, it was true …

"I just needed a fucking minute to gather my thoughts."

Frustrated at his predicament, he hadn't known what to feel, especially before she had walked in that door. After that night they had spent together on the yacht, he had been trying his damnedest to ignore her, even though it was impossible and proved itself so when it had blown up. Even the smallest interaction had him breaking his will, although he blamed it on the immense pressure and predicament they had landed in. Dante had told himself that he would figure it out when they got back to Kansas City, but she hadn't even given him a chance to do so. She had decided it all on her own, and sure, he should have been faster on the uptake, but it had been a long fucking time since he had been faced with these kinds of feelings, and he was rusty. It really wasn't until he had just watched her walk out that fucking door, and knowing his late wife, Melissa, would approve of her, that he finally accepted his feelings.

"What is that?" Leo asked, looking down at his desk to the folder.

Unfortunately, there was no hiding it, as his son had already seen her name at the top of the page. "I asked Sal for—"

"You didn't even need to do that," Leo hissed, knowing exactly what it was. "She would have told you anything you wanted to know about her, if you had fucking cared to ask."

He had been curious, as a father would be, with what they had talked about, and he had expected their conversation to be about Leo. He hadn't expected, however, the possibility they might've talked about her.

"So, that's what you two talked about? Nadia?'

"Partly," his son admitted, keeping the rest of their conversation hidden. "But if you finish reading that, you'll be making a mistake." He nodded toward the folder. "Whatever is in there, you should want to hear it from her."

Slowly, Dante closed the folder, knowing his son was right.

When a satisfied Leo went to leave his office, he quickly got out of his chair. "Son, wait."

Leo halted.

Meeting him on the other side, he stared down at his son. Out of all of his children, being around Leo hurt the most. Before the accident, it had hurt because he was the most like Melissa, his kindness and pure heart a constant reminder of what he had lost. After the accident, however, it hurt from how much he had changed. He no longer resembled Melissa, and that was what broke him, because now his choices had cost his son an eye, like it had cost his wife's life.

Looking into his ocean eye, he remembered Nadia's questions she had asked of Leo ...

"Do you plan on working for your father?"

"I used to think so."

"And now?"

"And now I don't know."

Dante had left the table because he had known exactly what his son's thoughts were, and he hadn't been a good enough father in the moment, but he wanted to try now.

"I want you to know that you could have lost both of your eyes, and I still would have found you a place in *the family*, if that's what you wanted."

Leo, even though he had too kind of a soul, had looked up to his older brothers. It had been their footsteps that he wanted to follow, not his father's. And while they all knew he wasn't built for the job before, him losing his eye was what made him think he couldn't join. Little did he know yet that was exactly why Leo was going to be made one day. He just didn't know it yet. Leo still needed to learn that he was no less than he was before. In actuality, he was greater. That, though, was going to be a long road for him to find out. Dante, however, was going to start doing everything in his power, as a father, for him now.

"Understand?" Dante asked when Leo simply stood there in shock from his words.

Leo finally nodded.

Reaching out, Dante did something he should have done every day since his wife's passing. He hugged his son. "I love you."

The rain that had yet to let up finally seemed to ease.

THE OLD WAYS

Nadia stood outside of Moonbeam's doors, looking at the black-tinted Cadillac that royally sucked at concealing itself. She made the slow journey to the car and knocked on the blacked-out window.

"I can see you two in there!" she roared. It might've been tinted to hell and back, but it wasn't impossible to see in with the sun out.

The window awkwardly dropped with the push of a button, and she couldn't help but laugh at the pair.

"I take it Dante sent you?" she asked the big one.

Amo spoke unapologetically, "Yep."

She looked to the blond one, who was still too young for this job. "Why are you here, then?"

Leo shrugged. "Thought I'd keep him company."

"Well ... at least make yourself useful." Nadia turned to walk back inside, but when they didn't begin following her, she looked back at them. "Come on, then."

Both car doors quickly opened following the cutting of the engine.

She left them behind, making them catch up to her in the small building.

"So, this is it?" Amo asked, confused.

"We're packing up." She smiled, knowing where his confusion was coming from. "And moving into a *huge* facility."

No thanks to Dante. She kept that part to herself. It was, however, Dante's friend, unbeknownst to her, she could thank. *Desmond Beck.* And Haley, of course, because he had made an offer in their meeting that Haley couldn't refuse. In return, he gave the plans to an abandoned mall here in Kansas City to be renovated into the next Moonbeam, becoming a self-sustainable community, with housing and jobs for all of her at-risk youth. It was a literal dream come true that only came at her friend's cost ... What that cost was, Nadia still hadn't been told. Haley promised to tell her when the time would come. She just prayed she would fare better than Nadia had with Dante.

"Oh." Amo looked around at all the teenagers helping to pack up. "Aren't some a little too old to be here?"

"I help kids up to nineteen years old. Just because you're eighteen and considered a legal adult doesn't mean you should stop receiving help." Those two years of being an adult were sometimes the hardest. You needed help to learn how to actually be an adult. By the time her kids reached twenty, they were set up for success in the real world.

She shook her head at seeing that Amo was pretty much uncomfortable here. The thought of a little work without receiving money clearly wasn't something he was interested in.

"How about you go help"—Nadia took a look around for the person whom she had in mind—"her."

"Her?" Amo asked, nodding to a girl who was struggling to hold up a huge box.

"Yep." Nadia smiled evilly and, thankfully, Amo had just missed it.

Leo, however, had not.

"You're doing something sneaky, aren't you?" he asked, watching Amo's back.

Nadia was caught by surprise. None of her evil plans were ever caught. Poor Haley had yet to even learn until it was too late. "How'd you know?"

"I don't need two eyes to know when someone's being a sneaky bastard." Leo smiled, letting her know he wasn't going to stop his friend from being ensnared in her trap. "Especially when you grew up with three of them."

"Well, you know what they say ..." She whistled, not even needing to say the last part, as both of them were well familiar with the saying.

Payback's a bitch.

F-o-r-g-i-v-e-n-e-s-s was an eleven-letter word that he was asking for from each of his children, and Leo had only been the beginning.

He stared at his children in front of him. His oldest, Lucca, stood in the corner, flipping the Zippo he had gifted him when he had become his underboss. The two chairs in front of his desk were occupied by his other children. Maria, his second oldest, he arguably owed the biggest apology to. Then Nero had followed her, but he was the first child whom he'd wronged.

"Thank you for coming to see me"—he specifically looked at Maria, who looked like she was going to leave any second—"even though I know I don't exactly deserve the chance to see you."

Unfortunately, the other two didn't have an option not to be here, as they worked for him.

Maria had stopped stirring at his words, finally looking up from the clock on her phone.

"And I don't think I should get the chance to explain myself, but I ask that you let me—"

"I am not listening to this shit again," Maria hissed, standing up and moving toward the door.

"Maria, please," he called out to her, hoping she would stop. Dante knew what she spoke of, and it was the exact reason she was so hurt by him.

The day she and Dominic Luciano had married had been the day that he had told his only daughter that he wouldn't be able to walk her down the aisle, let alone attend her wedding. He had tried his best to explain to her why, as the Caruso boss, he couldn't, but he, too, agreed it made him a poor excuse of a father.

"If you don't like what I have to say this time, you never have to see me again."

Maria paused but only went back to her seat when Lucca nodded for her to return.

"Thank you," he said gratefully.

It took him a moment and a long deep breath to put his words together. All three children shared something in common—they had all fallen hard in love with someone who wasn't of pure Italian blood. The single, oldest rule in the Italian mafia was that, in order to be made, you must be of pure Italian blood. Over the years, slight exceptions had been made that, as long as you were of mostly Italian descent, it was approved ... as long as you didn't have the Caruso name, that is. The men who bore the Caruso last name were ordered to keep their Italian blood pure. That way, the high positions they held in the family of boss and underboss were never taken from them.

The problem was that his children weren't the only ones who shared that commonality of falling hard for someone who wasn't of pure Italian blood.

"Your mother and I had an arranged marriage," he began the story they hadn't heard since they had been children. "Her father owned this casino hotel and had received many offers to sell, but the only way he would agree to sell to my father was if his daughter married his son. That way, when he passed, this property would pass to me, which would be returned back to his daughter, and then his future *grandchildren*." Dante stared at the faces of those grandchildren whom he spoke of before he got to the part that they had never been told before. "However, even though her father and mother were, in fact, Italian ... your mother was not."

This time when Lucca's Zippo flipped to a close, he didn't continue his movement of flipping it back open. "Who knows this?"

"Very few people ever did. Most of the ones who did are dead now." He knew his oldest son was the only one who knew the severity of this information, so he explained to Maria and Nero why he had disagreed with their choices in partners from the beginning. "If this information fell into the wrong hands, any future children you might have with *Dominic, Elle*, or *Chloe*"—he looked from Maria's emerald gaze to Nero's emerald pair then to the blue-green ones that glowed in the dark corner—"might never sit where I sit one day." They were already only fifty percent Italian, which meant Nero's and Lucca's children would only be twenty-five percent.

"Dom might be from Spanish descent, but he's fifty percent Italian," Maria told him, clearly not forgetting the conversation he'd had with her on her wedding day.

"Yes, but one day, you might be in the same position I'm in right now—worried about your future grandchildren."

She spoke to him as if he had forgotten a vital piece of information. "My children will be Lucianos."

"Yet you didn't take his last name?" Dante asked, raising a brow to look at the wedding ring that she so proudly wore on her finger. "The two families are starting to merge, and your children will not only carry Luciano blood, but Caruso as well. I imagine you will want them to at least have the chance to take their pick?"

Maria seemed to understand clearly now.

"Good thing you will be gone when that happens and the rules will have been changed," Nero finally spoke for the first time. His cold words reminding him that he might've been the first he wronged with more time to have passed, but he had yet to forget.

"There will always be those who will never forget the old ways." His grave warning was not only for Nero, but also his other children.

The silence was unquestionable, and it was only when he was certain his children finally understood that Nadia's words came to mind. *I have never come across anything that couldn't be fixed with a 'sorry' and some time.*

"I understand why you three might hate me forever, but I just wanted you to know it was never anything against who you three have chosen; it was my greed for power that kept me from accepting them like a father should have. I not only wanted my children to fill this seat one day, but I wanted your children and theirs after to fill this seat." Dante swallowed hard, having to clear his throat to say his final peace. "Otherwise, I feel like I would have lost your mother ... *Melissa*, for nothing."

It was the first time his children heard him speak her name since her death.

"I am sorry." He looked at each of them genuinely, but he now settled on Maria's green gaze that seemed to sparkle. "And I wish those words alone were enough to ask for forgiveness, but I can only hope you will give me the chance to prove just how sorry I am with time."

That sparkle in Maria's eyes had fallen as tears hit her cheeks. Not once had he seen his daughter cry, not even when her mother had died. Dante had passed on his lack of compassion and emotion to all of his children who were in the room.

"Shit." She wiped the tear away that was ruining her perfect makeup, as all of them stared at her in shock. "I'm pregnant."

Dante's heart skipped a beat. "Y-You are?"

"Yes." She cried glittering tears. "That's why I'm crying."

Throwing himself out of his chair, he practically ran over to his daughter and had to force himself to stop. "May I?" he asked, holding out his hand.

Maria stared at his tanned hand before taking it and placing it on her belly that was only just beginning to show. "It's a girl," she whispered through her tears.

Tears welled in his icy eyes. She could blame the tears on her pregnancy all she wanted, but he knew she was crying for the same reason he was, and she would soon find out ...

Little girls will always stay your little girl.

∞

Amo walked up to the girl holding the huge box that Nadia had pointed out. She looked like a fumbling box with a pair of legs as the only thing he could see of her was the short legs struggling to hold up the box she had just packed.

Ugh, he internally grumbled from having to be in here. He wished he were still in the car, just getting paid to watch Nadia, not getting paid to watch Nadia while actually having to do some work. Volunteering was something kids had to do to go to college, and even though Amo hadn't graduated high school that long ago, his ass still hadn't volunteered a day in his life because De Santis men didn't go to college. They went into the mafia to become made and were always the bodyguards of the highest decree, being the ones to guard the Caruso boss for generations. His uncle Drago had been one of the best of the De Santis protectors, and Amo was following in his footsteps.

When he got closer to her, she was just about to run into him before Amo rolled his eyes and bent down to take the box from her.

"Oh!" the girl huffed as the weight of the box was released from her. "Thank you."

"No problem," he grumbled under his breath.

"It goes over there, against the wall with the others."

Able to only see the top of her bright, orange hair, he sidestepped around her to move to the burgeoning pile of cardboard boxes.

"Wow, you're big—" The words slipped from her mouth in astonishment. "I mean, strong." She nervously laughed, correcting herself.

"Uh-huh," Amo said dismissively, hoping the kid would stop following him.

The girl didn't, however, clearly feeling the need to

explain her choice of words to him. She followed right behind him as she continued to nervously explain herself. "I'm sorry, I really didn't mean to call you big. You're just quite ..."

Amo walked faster, hoping she would take the fucking hint.

"Tall," she finally found the word. "Compared to me, is all."

She didn't, because weakening laughter still followed him.

"Because I'm, um ..."

He rolled his eyes again. *Short.*

"Short ..." she stated the obvious that clearly didn't need to be said but didn't know how stupid it sounded until she had said it. "I'm sorry. We should start again."

You see, this is exactly why I hate being around little kids. He threw the box down onto the pile and began to turn ... *They're fucking annoyi—*

"I'm Winnie."

Amo blinked at the girl smiling nervously up at him. Her voice had been so soft and sweet that he had thought she was just a little kid, but the girl didn't look that far in age from himself. And she was right; she was just short.

Able to see more than just her bright, orange hair, he moved his eyes to her button nose and chubby cheeks that were both just as rosy and covered in freckles. She looked like a cute, chubby bunny, and he figured she was about as harmless, too. While Amo looked like a beast that would swallow her whole in comparison.

He told himself to walk away, but the beast inside kept him in place.

Cause, oh ...

Did she look ...

Delicious.

Knowing it was just the hormones that had his daughter hugging him goodbye, along with hugging her other congratulating brothers, he watched her leave his office right before Nero gave him a nod. It might not have been a hug or an *I love you*, but he knew it was his son's way of forgiving him as he watched him, too, disappear through the door.

Dante hadn't expected much of a response from Lucca, so he wasn't surprised when he headed for the door without so much as a glance.

"Lucca ..." he said before he could walk through. "I'd like to talk to you alone for a moment."

Stopping, his son lightly closed the door before he walked over to take one of the leather chairs.

He watched Lucca reach into his pocket and pull out a pack of cigarettes. Putting the stick to his lips, he lit the end with the flick of his Zippo. Dante stared at the burning end. He had seen these exact motions a million times before, but never, not even once, had he slid the crystal ashtray he used for his cigars closer for him to use.

Lucca narrowed his eyes on the ashtray, unbelieving of the act himself.

"Son ..." Dante began the words he had been desperately holding on to, "it's time."

LAST FIRST KISS

Nadia waved the boys goodbye as she made it to her apartment door, fumbling with the keys for a moment before finally able to put it in the slot when the door opened.

"Hey, Nadia." Haley smiled mischievously.

That look caused Nadia to look past her to see Dante sitting on their couch behind her. *What the—*

"Bye, Nadia!"

"Where the hell are you going?" she asked as her friend passed her.

"Dante gave me a free room at his casino hotel for the night." Haley dangled a key out in front of her then yelled loud enough so her voice would travel, "Thanks again, Dante. I'll see you soon!"

Her mouth dropped open in disbelief and only dropped more when she watched her friend give her a thumbs-up of approval, along with a wink for good luck before she disappeared from view. Unlike Nadia, Haley wasn't above gambling, especially when it came to playing slots, as it was the perfect loner activity.

"What the fuck?" Nadia spoke the rest of her thought rather than thinking it.

"What?" Dante asked, confused from where he sat in the small living area.

"She doesn't ..." She had to replay what she had just witnessed in her mind before she could finish. "Haley doesn't talk to people."

"Sure she does. She just did."

"Not if she can help it," she explained while she came inside and closed the door behind her. "And she certainly doesn't talk to strangers, let alone men who come to our apartment uninvited."

"Hm ..." Dante brushed it off, seeing it wasn't a big deal. *But it is.* "She likes you."

"I take it that's a big deal, too?"

"Yes, she's not exactly a people person," Nadia said, looking at him curiously now. It was like she was trying to figure out what the hell Haley saw in him to be able to talk to him like it was nothing.

"Neither am I." He shrugged. "Maybe that's why."

"And what about her?" she asked, crossing her arms. "Did you like Haley?"

It was clear he didn't know how to respond based on her stance. "She's ... nice?"

Her eyes went into slits. "Just nice?"

"Yeah, she was nice, woman! I only got to talk to her for ten minutes before you walked in the door. What the fuck else do you want me to say? Other than I can certainly see why you two get along."

Dante was rethinking this whole fucking thing. The headache this was already causing was the exact reason he had never wanted another relationship in his life. And hell, they weren't even in a fucking relationship. He was fucking here to try to see if they could start one, and it was already going bad from having to dodge around and answer the stupid-ass questions properly that women always asked.

The only reason he wasn't walking out that door right now was because the woman had brought his children back into his life.

"How's that?"

"For one, she's the only one I've seen who's been able to stop your roll." Dante was fucking envious of Haley for that. Nadia had controlled the endings of all their conversations as of late, yet her friend, who was supposedly meek and mild, had controlled theirs.

"No, she places speed bumps, so I never get lost." Quietly, Nadia took a seat beside him on the couch.

Dante watched her mouth open to say something else, but then she closed it, deciding not to. "What were you going to say?"

Nadia had to clear the sorrow out of her throat before she could begin. "My father killed my mother when I was child. If I hadn't hidden in the laundry hamper, he would have killed me, too."

His son had been right; she so freely started to give her story away, so there was no need to search for it anywhere else. The contents of that folder would have never been as rewarding to know as she continued.

"I was so petrified he was going to find me that I wouldn't breathe. Then I smelled smoke and heard another gunshot. The smoke made it harder for me to stay quiet as I started to feel myself choking. If I hadn't been afraid he would hear me coughing, I wouldn't have jumped out of the hamper and started running.

"I thought, if I could just make it to the door, I could get help for my mom. I remember it being so smoky that I couldn't see where I was going. The firefighter who rescued me found me a few inches away from the door. My father must have heard the sirens and shot himself." She paused briefly, then her tone returned quieter. "You know the sickest part?"

"No." The Mafioso didn't want to, either. He wouldn't be able to make the son of a bitch pay for whatever Nadia was about tell him. If the man were alive, Dante wouldn't even order the hit. He would have done the job himself.

"Even when I found out my mother was dead, I hated him just as much for killing himself. I was left with no one. No one who would care how I was treated in foster care. No one who would care if I was lonely. No one who would answer a call in the middle of night if my car broke down."

Dante finally understood what Nadia was explaining to him before she even did. "Haley would pick up the phone."

She nodded, glad he understood. "Haley bought me my first cell phone. I've had people ask me why I'm friends with her. I say the same thing every time. I can't understand why she's friends with me."

He reached out to take her hand with his tanned one. "How do they respond?"

She curled her fingers, holding his back. "I don't know, because I leave after saying it and cut them out of my life."

"That's why you asked me what I thought of her." Dante now smiled, expecting no less from her. "You were prepared to cut me out of your life if I said the wrong thing."

"It would have been a deal breaker, yes." Nadia smiled back, not making any apology for her feelings.

His breath hitched in his throat at the sight. "Well, in that case, I like her ... almost as much as I like you."

"Oh, really?" Nadia snuggled closer to him on the couch.

"Mmhmm ..." Dante chuckled, letting his lips get closer to hers. "A lot."

"Well, I like you, too," she breathed.

He moved his lips closer. "How much?"

"A lot."

He captured her lips; it was the first kiss he'd had in years, and this time, he hoped it would be the last first kiss he would ever have to give ...

THE KISS WAS MORE THAN SHE COULD HAVE DREAMED of. She knew it wasn't something he so freely gave. He had given his body to her that night on the yacht, but never as an act of love, like the hand held in hers or a simple kiss. That was something she knew he held tightly in his heart, only ever given to his wife.

Deepening the kiss, Nadia was too afraid he would change his mind and pull away, so she positioned herself on his lap, hoping it would hold him there with her forever.

However, it would be Nadia who had the sense knocked into her.

Pulling her lips away, she was able to think clearly. "Wait. I meant when I said we can't ever even start *whatever this is* ... I can't find out what it's like to have you in my life, only to lose you."

He snuck another kiss on her lips. "Well, it's a good thing I gave it up, then."

"You what?" she asked, pulling her face back to look at him.

"I let Lucca have what he's always wanted," Dante said, as if the words weren't a big deal.

She knew better to know that they were a big deal. It was obvious *the family* had been the only thing Dante truly cared about for years. "I-I can't have you doing that for me."

"I didn't do it for you ... I did it for me."

Her heart melted into a puddle, much like she was becoming in his arms with each word he spoke.

Dante's ice-blue eyes seemed to slowly defrost. "I can't bury another woman in my life because of my choices. I will not allow it."

"Oh. That changes things," Nadia said breathlessly when he lifted her up and walked them to her room. She felt his strength with the ease he carried her. Dante Caruso was an indomitable man. He was used to wielding his power in Kansas City, and Nadia had seen people cower when his name was mentioned.

Had she been swayed with the attraction she was feeling to accept him so easily into her life just because he said he was letting his son take over for him?

"I don't like that look on your face."

Nadia didn't try to hide her trepidation.

"You're lucky Haley likes you, or I wouldn't have let you in the door. I would have made you at least take me out to dinner a couple of times. I don't want you to think I'm easy because I slept with you so quickly."

Putting her down, Dante started rolling her pants and thong over her hips until they puddled at her feet. Removing her top, he let it drop carelessly to the floor onto the growing pile. Placing a hand on her waist, he then started pushing her backward. "There is nothing easy about what you do to me," he said, giving her another push so she toppled to the bed.

Languidly, Nadia watched as Dante divested himself of his clothes until there was nothing for them to hide behind. Normally, the times she had sex, she had felt self-conscious with her nudity. For some unexplainable reason, she didn't with Dante. The male appreciation in his gaze brought a warm heat to her groin without him having to lay so much as a finger on her.

"Mr. Caruso, surely you don't think I'm naïve enough to believe that you don't have women trying to get your attention regularly." She remembered the unanswered text message he had received and doubted it had been his first.

Dante grinned, running a finger from her collarbone to the valley between her breasts, riding the swell to the rosy patch of color. He used the pad of his thumb to trace the areola, bringing it to a pert tip.

"Striving and getting are two different horses. I prefer thoroughbreds, and I don't come in contact with those frequently."

Ah, so that was why he didn't care if she gambled in his casino. He was a horse-betting guy.

Leaning over her, Dante licked the tip he had awakened.

"Are you comparing me to a horse?" She laughed.

"Oh, darling ... there are worse things to complain about than being compared to a thoroughbred. I should know. I can spot a winner a mile away."

Goose bumps broke out on her skin when Dante blew a small puff of air on the wet tip.

"Uh, I wasn't complaining ... believe me." She gave a small moan when he moved his mouth to her other nipple.

"You taste like sunlight." He traveled back to the valley

between her breasts to move upward to her chin, then hovered over her lips. Nadia caught conflicting emotions cross his face before he lowered his mouth over hers.

Shamelessly, she pulled him down over her. She had never wanted to become lost in a man the way she did with Dante. There was a darkness about him that made her believe the dangerous reputation he had earned had been based on fact and not overblown gossip.

His mouth clung to hers like a leaf floating down a river to see where it would go. There was something both vulnerable and earnest about the way he was kissing her that it sowed a seed of a possible future between them.

He wasn't treating her like a one-night stand, like he had the first time. No, he was treating her with the care and attention of a man who wanted to protect something precious.

Their kiss went from exploring to passionate when Dante's hips sank harder on hers. Every movement he made heightened her awareness of what he was doing to her body.

Reaching out a hand, he took hers to lift it over her head, stretching her body taut under him. Nadia licked her bottom lip to taste him on the silky skin. Moving with a natural sexiness that showed his raw masculinity, Dante plunged his cock inside her. He didn't have to check to see if she was wet for him. He knew.

As he seated himself to the hilt in one long, smooth motion, she cried out in ecstasy at the feelings he was creating. There wasn't anything magical or dreamlike about what Dante was doing to her. His more dominate personality claiming her in a sensuous glide of flesh meeting flesh in the endeavor to achieve the fleeting moment of rapture, he wanted to give to her and take for himself.

Fervently, Nadia responded in the only way she could—

by surrendering instead of fighting the rise of the tide that was threatening to overtake her.

His mouth returned to hers as his thrusts gained speed, like the leaf that was now traveling through rough waters. She held on, going where Dante was leading her, clinging to his shoulders for dear life, determined to hang on for each precious moment. Dante was unrelenting, like a never-ending rapid she didn't think would ever end. Then, in one single burst, she found herself going over a waterfall to fall safely back to Earth with Dante murmuring in her ear and stroking her body in soothing movements that showed it was safe to breathe once again. Thank God she had been drunk when they'd had sex the first time, or when she had gone to his office, she would have latched on to him. Not even Amo would have been able to pull her off him.

"Am I alive?" she gasped out.

Dante gave a growling laugh against her throat. "Yes."

"I can see why everyone says you're lethal. I thought I was about to go through Heaven's gate there for a second."

"Only a second? Damn."

"Any longer, and you would have needed to bring me back to life."

Dante reached a long arm down to the floor to pick up the blanket that had fallen, covering them as he settled down next to her. "You have any plans for tomorrow?"

Raising sleepy eyes to his, she saw he had risen up on one elbow. "Nothing in particular."

"Feel like hanging out with me for a few days at the beach?"

"There's a beach in Kansas City?" she asked, trying not to yawn.

"I was thinking more like Cancun."

Contentedly, she placed her head in the curve of his arm, snuggling closer to him. "How long?"

"A couple of weeks, maybe three."

Nadia instinctively knew why he wanted to go on a sudden trip after the one they just had. He wanted her far enough away from One-Shot until his son Lucca either unmasked the person or killed them.

"I'll have to ask Haley."

"I already did. She said she didn't see any problems she couldn't handle."

"I don't know if I'm liking this relationship you are developing with my best friend." However, she could see how important it was to him that she was out of harm's way. "But I'll go as long as I don't have to get on any boats."

"We'll fly there," he said, finally able to relax since she said she would come. "Desmond has a private jet. I'll ask if he'll fly us there."

Nadia made a comical face at him. "Good luck with that. I wouldn't even place a one-dollar bet on that possibility."

He disagreed. "He owes me a couple more favors."

"Dante, I hate to be the bearer of bad news, but I think any favors he owed you were blown to hell and back."

D ante skirted around the workmen carrying plywood and tools inside the mall that Nadia was converting into Moonbeam. Glancing around the bustle of activity taking place, he searched for Nadia.

Amo had texted him to explain which portion of the mall Nadia was currently working in. Taking his phone, he was about to text Amo back to ask for better directions, when he heard a laugh coming from somewhere above his head. Recognizing the joyful sound coming from the ceiling, he moved forward and looked up then nearly lost his lunch.

Nadia was balanced on one board between two scaffolds, walking on the thin plank as if she were a fucking gymnast. Dante lost ten years off his life at seeing her casually hanging a "Welcome" banner from the ceiling.

Afraid to take his eyes off her, he started making his way toward one of the scaffolds.

How in the fuck did she even get up there?

Terrified that if he said something, she would lose her balance, he snarled at two workers who were walking past him, in too big of hurry to get where they were going to pay any attention to him. He lost another five years of his life when the long sheet of plywood they were carrying came within a hairsbreadth of hitting one of the scaffolds that Nadia was on.

Silently reciting the rosary, Dante finally reached one of the scaffolds, trying to determine how to get up the fucking thing.

"I'm up here, Dante!"

Jumping in his shoes at Nadia yelling down at him, he managed to choke down the hellfire he was going to bring down on her head once she was on firm ground again.

"Having fun?" he asked blandly.

"We're having a blast!" She smiled, completely unaware of his feelings. "Amo and Leo are around the corner, if you're looking for them."

It was everything he could do to stay cool. "I came to see you. Can you come down here so we can talk?"

Nadia leaned over the side to frown down at him. "I'm a bit bus—"

"It's important," he urged as ice-cold fear had him promising to seek the nearest confessional right after he turned her ass the same color as the red-hot rage streaking through him. "How did you get up there?"

"I climbed." She lightly walked to the side of the plank farther away from him, and he saw her swing a leg over the metal bar and begin to climb down.

Swiftly, he went to hold the bottom of the ladder that had been hidden from his view by a large pillar.

She jumped down the last two steps, then Nadia's jubilation collided full force with his fear.

Taking her by the arms, he jerked her into his. "What in the fuck were you thinking to be up there? You could have broken your neck," he blasted her. "I told you I didn't want to lose another woman I love, and you're up there, prancing around like you're going to win the gold medal on the balance beam!"

"I-I'm sorry." Nadia snuggled into his chest instead of pushing away. "I didn't mean to scare you."

"Scare me? You took ten years off my life, and you're going to pay me back for each one of them."

"How am I supposed to do that?" she asked politely, twining her arms around his waist.

"I want us to go away for a couple of weeks."

Nadia shook her head. "Look around. This is a madhouse."

"Haley can take care of anything that needs to be taken care of."

"That's true," she said after a few moments of thinking. "To tell you the truth, I think she would rather I disappear so I will quit spending money."

"So, you'll go?" he asked hopefully.

"Depends. I have no desire to get on a boat ever again. The last time, we almost got blown to smithereens."

"We could fly to a Greek island?" he suggested. "Desmond has a plane."

Nadia laughed. "I don't see him letting you borrow it anytime soon."

"I'm sure he would."

"I wish I could be a fly on a wall for that conversation." Raising her chin from his chest, she gave him a critical glance. "You really were worried about me, weren't you?"

"How could you tell?"

"You haven't let me go, and everyone is standing around, watching us. I think some of the workers are afraid for me."

Dante shot an icy glare around at the onlookers. "I wouldn't hurt a hair on your head."

"I didn't think you would." Using her shoulder, she nudged him to turn to the side. "You want a tour?" When he still didn't let her go, she nudged him again. "Come on. I want your opinion on an idea I have."

Dante tried to pay attention as Nadia pointed out several areas where the workers were making repairs, or the changes Nadia and Haley wanted. Concentrating was difficult because he still was picturing Nadia carefree walking on the plank feet above the floor. One small slip, and Nadia could have been seriously hurt, if not killed.

He was unable to take his eyes off her as she explained Moonbeam's future plans, and all he could think was that all those future plans would have been snuffed out with one slip of her tennis shoe.

The realization he had come full circle with Nadia overlapping the love he had shared with Melissa slapped him in the face. Neither circle was stronger or weaker than the other. He would be just as lost if Nadia had fallen as he had when he had lost Melissa. Love couldn't be measured by length or depth. No, what he was feeling was more intrinsic and simpler than that. The other person's happiness had to go above your own. He had been a selfish, stingy bastard even before Melissa's death, and it had only grown worse afterward.

Having Nadia walk away from him because she refused to accept any potential thing that could bring unhappiness to her life was a self-defense mechanism she put in due to her childhood. You could see she only wanted to start each day with a smile, and regardless of how tired she was at the end of the day, she only wanted it ending with a smile, too.

"This is the area I wanted to show you."

Dante saw a group of construction workers had taken out a portion of the wall to install doors. Carefully, they walked over lumber to make their way outside.

The area sat snugly between two curves of the mall. Each of those curves had their own separate exits. There were even more workers out here. Another wall was being built opposite of the one they had gone through.

"This is going to be our tranquility garden. The kids can come out here to relax, or just to have some time alone." Nadia grabbed his hand. "I want to plant different types of trees here. The ceiling is going to be like a conservatory, so they'll be able to sit outside despite the weather. Can you imagine sitting out here in the winter when it's snowing?" she asked breathlessly.

He actually could.

"It'll be beautiful." Dante imagined the area filled with trees and kids using the opportunity to unwind.

"I think so, too. We're going to use artificial turf so they'll be able to sit and have picnics, even when it's freezing outside. I get a tingle inside just thinking about what it will look like when it's done. In the middle, we're going to have a big pine tree so all of the kids living here can help decorate it during the holiday."

Dante saw hesitation in her gaze when she turned back to him.

"With your permission, we'd like to call this area the Melissa Caruso Tranquility Garden?"

The tightness in his throat prevented him to speak the words for a moment, "She would like that."

"I thought I would ask Lucca for help to know what flowers and trees to plant."

He could only nod his head, knowing Lucca had brought Melissa's garden, which he had let die, back to life.

"I would appreciate any help he or any of your children would be willing to give." Linking her arm through his, she proudly beamed at the work that was taking place in front of her. "I want the garden to reflect how much you and her children loved her."

Dante placed a gentle kiss on her lips. "That isn't all it will reflect."

"What do you mean?"

Wistfully, he stared into her eyes. "It will show how much love and dedication you put into Moonbeam. You give everything. You never measure the cost to you. You just give all of yourself. Even to me when you said you wouldn't. You caved after just one kiss. You share your heart with everyone you come into contact with."

She lovingly wrapped her arms around his neck. "What can I say? I'm easy."

He didn't laugh at her humor. "Just do me a favor and don't get on anything above four feet."

Surprise showed on her face. "You were that scared for me?"

"Put it this way, I made two promises when I saw you up there: go to confessional to confess my sins ... and tell you I love you."

"I was perfectly safe, Dante—" Realization hit her at what he had just said. "You love me?"

He nodded, having only been this sure once before. Like what this room would one day hold, Dante had a woman who smelled of flowers, and now a woman who smelled of sunlight. That was why he had been so attracted to Nadia's scent; it was so different from Melissa's, but it was the exact thing you needed for flowers to grow. Whereas a flower's time would come to a beautiful end, the sun was always there to greet you in the morning.

And it was clear his sun had been waiting for this day and wanted to cherish it.

"How much?"

Dante smiled. "A lot."

"I love you, too," she said the words that he, too, had been waiting to hear. However, it was obvious from the heat that continued to radiate off him that he was still unhappy she had been up there. "I swear I've been much higher than that before. There was nothing to worry over."

Dante felt himself breaking out in a cold sweat. "If that's supposed to make me feel better, it doesn't."

"If it means that much to you, my feet will stay firmly planted on the ground from now on. I promise."

Dante gave a sigh of relief. No arguments, nothing except the agreement that she wouldn't put him in that position of fear again.

"You know, I've never begged for anything my whole life, not from any man, woman, or even God have I considered lowering my pride for. Darling, I was getting ready to beg you for that promise."

"Now you don't have to. You won't ever have to with me, Dante." Her words slipped from her lips like an oath. "Anything you want from me, all you have to do is ask."

"Then are we going to take that vacation I wanted to?"

"Yes," she laughingly agreed. "But I still say Desmond won't fly us there. He wouldn't let us near his plane and made us fly commercial to Cancun."

"This is different. I plan to give him a good reason."

Slight concern showed on her face. "Like what? Is there someone else who wants to kill us?"

"No. We're going to be celebrating."

"What will we be celebrating?" She frowned,

wondering if an occasion had slipped her mind. "Neither of our birthdays are near."

Knowing Dante had fulfilled the promise to his late wife, he was now finally ready to move on with his life and make a new promise. "Our honeymoon."

EPILOGUE 2
MAKING WINE FROM SUNSHINE

A bout to get into the car, she saw Dante come through the Caruso family home gate.

"Give me a sec, Maria." Nadia closed the car door instead of getting inside. "I just want to tell Dante when I'll be back."

Narrowing her eyes, she took note of what Dante was wearing as he stepped out of the Cadillac.

"I hoped to catch you before you left," he said as she approached him.

Nadia didn't miss the guilty look in his eyes as she brushed a kiss on his firm lips. "You got here just in time. Wait—why are you wearing a different suit than you left wearing a couple of hours ago?"

"Amo spilled his coffee on me. I changed into the extra suit I keep at the Casino Hotel."

She took a few steps back from him. "That's the third time in three weeks you've had to change your suits because of an accident."

Dante gave her an incredulous look. "You don't think I

have to change because I'm afraid you'll smell another woman's perfume on me, do you?"

"No." She folded her arms over her chest. "What I think is that you smoked one of your nasty cigars there, and you're trying to hide the evidence."

"Nadia ..."

"Dante ..." she mocked him back. "I tasted the cigar on your lips. I told you I don't mind if you smoke the occasional cigars, so there's no need to go to this extreme to hide that you are."

"I told you I'd quit before our wedding, and I will"—he ran a hand through his thick hair that was peppered with gray more and more each day—"try."

Nadia reached out to kiss him again much longer this time, not able to resist the stubborn look on his face. "I'm sure you will," she fibbed, both of them knowing he probably wouldn't, but it didn't much matter to her. She was certain Dante used that time to reminisce in his old office and check in on the family business. "Maria, Winnie, and I are going for the final fitting of my wedding dress. I shouldn't be gone long."

He frowned at her. "You girls aren't going alone, are you?"

Striding away, she blew him a kiss from over her shoulder. "We'll be fine"

"Take my car. Amo will drive yo—"

"You really want Amo tagging along?" she asked, getting in the car. One last look at his face told her he, in fact, did not.

Putting the car in drive, her head was flung back onto the headrest as Maria pressed her heel on top of her foot to speed them away from the house.

"Maria!" she screamed out, regaining control of the car. "We're not in an F1 race."

"I'm not getting stuck with someone looking over our shoulders. It's a girls' day out, and that means no men."

Since she hadn't wanted any men to spoil the day either, she didn't argue. With One-Shot revealed, and the two mafia families no longer feuding, it meant the girls could get a day to themselves on the rare occasion from time to time. However, Nadia was certain they were going to have a tail before they made it to their destination, regardless of how fast Maria was making her drive.

"What's on the agenda? As long as we're at the dress shop by three, we can go anywhere."

"I made us an appointment at my spa. We're going to be groomed and spoiled today. We probably won't want to go home by the time they are done with us."

Her and Maria shared a secretive women's glance, knowing nothing would keep them from going home to their men other than an act of God.

At the spa, she was treated to a wax, nails done and, saving the best for last, a full body massage. Meeting up at the swimming pool, they relaxed on lounge chairs, each of them wiggling their toes to show off their new polish.

Sipping on their mimosas, Winnie sipped on a non-acholic fruity concoctions, which was better than what her and Maria were drinking.

"How's the job hunting going, Winnie?" Nadia asked, wishing she hadn't after seeing the worried expression replace the happy one on her friend's sweet face.

"Not so good." Her head hung low in embarrassment. "I've put in over twenty applications, and I haven't been asked for a single interview."

Winnie had actively been looking for a job to support herself since turning eighteen. She shared a room with another girl who had run away from home and had ended up at Moonbeam, as well. Once Willow left, another runaway would be given her spot.

"I feel bad. You've already let me stay six months longer than I should have."

"Regardless of age, Haley and I want the residents to have a good environment to go to before leaving. You help us out so much; I wish you would stay and take the job we offered you as being an advisor to the other girls while you go to school."

"I don't want to go to college or do any other training courses until I'm certain I know what I want to do."

Nadia wasn't surprised at Winnie not wanting to stay at Moonbeam or being an advisor. Winnie was great with the other girls; the problem was the girls all loved Winnie, seeing her as a surrogate sister, which activated her flight response.

"I could talk to Haley and see if we could make an exception for you."

Winnie shook her head. "I don't want you to. I know I should take one of the training courses offered." She sighed morosely. "I just want to get on my feet and make enough money for a small place to live and be on my own for a while."

"I understand." Willow had a good head on her shoulders. She was undecided in her future, and she didn't want to jump into a field she would be unhappy with just to keep a roof over her head. "I'll talk to Dante; maybe he could find a job for you at the casino."

"I'd save that talk for when Winnie turns twenty-one," Maria spoke up. "Unless they're family, they aren't getting through the hiring process."

Without thinking, Nadia responded to Maria's quick dismissal of her idea. "Winnie *is* family to me."

She could have smacked herself when the poor girl hastily excused herself to get dressed, while Maria watched her leave in confusion.

"Why did she take off? We have plenty time before we have to leave."

"Winnie isn't comfortable showing her emotions. She doesn't want to get attached to anyone, and if anyone gets too close to her, she distances herself from them."

Maria arched a perfect brow at her. "Then why did you tell her you consider her family?"

"It was a slip of the tongue. I know better." Regretfully, she wished she could replay the last couple of minutes and not have brought up her searching for a job.

"I don't know how you do it. You play mother to I don't know how many kids. I do well just getting Angelica to bed at night at a decent hour. On top of that, you have to deal with their emotional issues. It must be disheartening at times."

Nadia gurgled the end of her mimosa and laughed. "If I was afraid of getting the cold shoulder from someone emotionally closed off, I wouldn't be engaged."

"Poor Dante. He didn't stand a chance against you, did he?" Maria said, giving her an appreciative look.

She put a finger to her lips. "Don't tell him. He thinks he caught me."

They were still laughing when Winnie came back.

"I guess we should go." Nadia rose from the lounge chair lazily. "We should get some lunch before going to the dress shop."

GOING TO ONE OF HER FAVORITE LUNCH SPOTS, THEY chatted about the wedding until it was time to go to the dress shop.

Trying her dress on was a more emotional experience than she had expected. Looking at herself in the mirror, her eyes met Maria's bedazzling emerald gaze.

"You look beautiful."

Nadia bit her lip. It had to be hard on Maria seeing her in the wedding dress, yet Dante's daughter only showed happiness for her. "Thank you, Maria."

Suddenly, Maria frowned. "What for?"

Taking a step toward her, she held open her arms. "Can I hug you?"

Her frown turned to confusion. "Do you have to?"

"I'd like to," she said, taking no offense. The beautiful woman hardly ever showed any emotion and had many familiar traits to her older brother Lucca.

"Then go ahead," she finally agreed.

Nadia enfolded Maria in her arms, letting all the love she felt for her come out in a motherly hug. After a moment, she stepped back. "Thank you. I needed that."

Maria's eyes held a faint shimmer of tears, realizing just how truly special and gifted of a woman her father was marrying. "I think I did, too."

After dropping off Winnie, Nadia was ready to go home, already thinking ahead to what she would prepare for dinner. With her mind on her chances of getting Dante to grill steaks, she didn't find Maria's request strange.

"Have you seen the house next door?"

"No." She hadn't actually. Massive trees interrupted the vision of being able to see the home.

"Do me a favor and pull into the driveway."

Doing as she was asked since now she was intrigued herself, Nadia could only see a massive fence barring further entrance to the estate.

Spitting off a series of numbers, Nadia was shocked. "How do you know the gate code?"

"I know the owner." Maira shrugged it off before getting her to put the code into the keypad.

Driving up the large driveway, Nadia's first glance at the home had her mouth dropping. The home was smaller than the Caruso family home, but it held a charm the austere appearance of the Caruso home did not. "This is gorgeous."

"I thought you'd like it." Maria's lips held a smug smile. "You want to check it out?"

Nadia gave her a surprised glance. "The owners won't mind us showing up unexpectedly?"

"They won't. The Hendersons are on vacation. Dante told them he'd keep an eye on the property while they're gone. We'll be saving him a trip over."

"If you're sure, then hell yes." No woman in her right mind wouldn't take a look inside.

Eagerly getting out of the car, they entered the house. Nadia had to suck in a breath. With the layout a smaller version as well of the Caruso home, the entryway was breathtaking with a beautiful staircase and living room off to the side that held the same charm as the outside. The furniture was a mixture of different shades of creams and blues that somewhat reminded her of the multi-million-dollar yacht her and Dante had been on before it had blown up. If she didn't know Desmond Beck didn't own this home, considering Haley was now happily married to him, she'd almost think it was his and not the Hendersons.

"Wow, they must have spent a fortune on an interior decorator."

"Thank you."

Maria's words had her turning her head toward her. "*You* did this?"

Proudly, Maria nodded.

"Maria ... this is ... beautiful." Awestruck, Nadia didn't know what else to say.

"What do you think?"

Spinning at hearing Dante's question, she saw him standing behind her.

"Did you come to check out the house for your neighbors? Maria tried to save you a trip."

Father and daughter shared a strange look before Maria turned back to her. "Since Dante is here, I better get home and save Matthais from his niece."

"You didn't answer my question," Dante said once his daughter had left them alone. "What do you think of the house?"

"It's gorgeous. Your neighbors hit the jackpot when Maria agreed to decorate it for them."

"Maria didn't decorate the house for the Hendersons," Dante said, clearing his throat. "She decorated it for us."

"I don't understand," Nadia said in confusion.

"This is our new home. I bought this home as a wedding present to you." Dante walked further into the living room, dominating the space with his mere presence. "With Lucca taking over, and him and Chloe starting a family of their own, it's time for them to create their own memories while we begin creating our own, as well."

Rushing toward Dante, she wrapped her arms around his waist. "You didn't have to give me such a big home."

"I like space." He shrugged. "Once Leo goes back to school, this place will be a madhouse with the friends he'll invite over. At least it was before he was injured."

Nadia pressed her fingers over his lips. "You're not going to go there. You can't blame yourself for someone else's actions."

Feeling the tension ebb out of Dante's muscled body, she tilted her head back. "Are you going to show me the rest of our new home?"

With them going hand in hand, they went through the sliding door to the outside where there was an outdoor kitchen as well as a television area with cozy outdoor furnishings. Several feet away there was a pool, which had a huge gate-blocking entry that would be safe for his future grandchildren.

Going back inside, they went into the kitchen, which she was pretty sure she was going to have to have lessons on how to work the equipment.

The upstairs was decorated just as amazingly, as Dante showed her Leo's room.

"He's going to move his things in here before we come back from our honeymoon."

Feeling warm inside from everything falling into place, they went inside the last room he was clearly waiting to show her.

Walking inside, she stared at the room in confusion. "Did Maria not get to this one yet?"

"She's going to come by in the morning so you two can go furniture shopping. Our room will be finished before we get back. You'll have to pick the paint color you want, too."

Nadia liked the sound of being able to add her own personal touch to their bedroom, but she had a feeling that, with both of them designing a room together, they could do some serious damage. "What's my budget?"

"Whatever makes you happy."

"I knew there was a reason I loved you so much," she said, sauntering over to him.

"Only one?" he teased.

"There might be a few other things I love about you." Hugging him by his neck, she gave him a slow smile. "How understanding you are about my job, and how much you know the kids mean to me ..."

Dante's eyes narrowed on her suspiciously. "What do you want now?"

Damn. He was good. There was never no buttering up the ex-king of Kansas City.

"Winnie needs a job."

"You look beautiful, Nadia."

Grinning at her best friend, she dabbed at her eyes with a tissue, careful not to smear her makeup. "I hope Dante will think so."

"I'm sure he will." Taking the tissue away, Haley fixed her makeup. "There. You can't even tell you cried."

"Thank you," she said, trying her best to keep her tears inside from now on.

"Are you ready to go up? We should have been up there five minutes ago." Giving Nadia her bouquet, as well as taking her own, Haley urged her out of the master suite.

"Thank you again for talking Desmond into letting us have the wedding on his brand-new yacht and for letting us take it for our honeymoon." She had to admit it was much better than their original thought of just flying to Cancun.

"Just promise me this time it comes back in one piece, or he'll divorce me." Haley's laughter told her she was only teasing.

"I promise. Dante handpicked the crew himself this time." Reaching the top level, she heard music playing and a knot instantly grew in her stomach.

They had only invited family and a few close friends. The main deck had been decorated with flowers and had an arch where Dante and her would take their vows. Their reception would be on the upper deck once the ceremony was over.

"Dante is here, isn't he?" she asked, too afraid to look.

"Of course he is," Haley calmly assured her. "He's standing next to Desmond."

Nadia gave a shaky sigh of relief. "I was afraid he would change his mind at the last minute." Nadia gripped Haley's arm nervously. "I never expected to love someone as much as I do him."

"I'm not surprised. You're the kindest person I know. You made me your friend when I had no one. You make sure dozens of children are safe and have a safe roof over their heads, with food to eat. You deserve every ounce of love Dante showers on you."

"Don't make me cry again." She sniffled back the tears at what Haley had said.

"Then I suggest we go get you married while you still have some mascara on."

To say that their ceremony was everything she had always wanted was an understatement. The most meaningful moment to her was when she saw a sheen gloss over Dante's icy eyes while he said his vows as the orange sun was setting behind him. It would be a moment she would never forget, not even in her final dying breath.

With their reception lasting well into the early morning, they left after saying goodbye to their fun-fueled guests and headed down to their room. Exhausted from the festivities, they passed out on the bed, and when she woke, she found herself laying on top of Dante's chest.

"What time is it?" she asked groggily.

Stirring next to her, Dante looked at his phone. "Don't ask."

Nadia tried to raise her head only to have to lower it back down at the stinging sensation. "I think my hair is stuck to the headboard."

Shifting upward, Dante turned on the light. "How much hairspray did you use?"

"Don't ask," she replied with a laugh.

After Dante detangled her hair for her, she shimmied out of the bed.

"I have to go take a shower to wash my hair and get this makeup off."

"You want some company?" he asked, smiling, clearly reminiscing about the first night they had slept together.

"Are you going to behave yourself?"

He shrugged. "Probably not."

Expecting as much, she winked. "Then come on."

Going into the bathroom, she removed the panty set she

had been wearing when she had taken off her wedding dress while Dante started the water for her.

The slightly warm water was refreshing, and with Dante helping her wash her hair, it didn't take long before she felt half-human again.

"I was afraid you wouldn't show up," she said, pressing kisses along his collarbone only to have him booming with laughter.

"I had Amo stationed outside your door to make sure you didn't run off."

Joining in on the chuckling, she was thinking how perfectly they matched when Dante suddenly left her in the shower. She turned the shower water off to see that her husband was starting a bath.

"Exactly what are you planning, Mr. Caruso?" she asked with a reminiscing smile of her own.

Stepping into the luxurious tub foaming with the Sunshine Kisses bubble bath, he sat down before he held out a hand to help his wife carefully inside. Waiting until she snugly fit in front of him, he curled two palms over her breasts and pulled her back to his chest.

"Making wine from sunshine, Mrs. Caruso."

GOODBYE

i said we were over a Gazillion times,
but even i didn't believe my Own mind.
if Only you had stayed the same,
as the Day that i had met you,
you'd still Be mine.
but now i'll never forgive You,
for making me put the E in goodbye.

SARAH BRIANNE

Please, if you or someone you know ever needs help,
follow this link to get more information and help.

YOU ARE NOT ALONE.

victimsofcrime.org

www.ingramcontent.com/pod-product-compliance
Lightning Source LLC
Chambersburg PA
CBHW071312250626
47159CB00004B/1390